I0788136

The Lies We Lived

Eve Campbell

Cover By Anna Neiman (AllenariBookCovers)

ISBN-9781923416079

Chapter One

Matteo

The nightclub's a fucking warzone of sound and sin, lights strobe like gunfire, bass pounding like a heartbeat that's about to flatline. Smoke coils through the air, thick as secrets, laced with sweat, sex, and the sting of cheap liquor.

I couldn't give a single shit about the bodies writhing out there on the dancefloor, they're noise, static, nothing.

I'm not here to dance. I'm not here to feel.

I'm here to forget.

To fuck.

To bleed the poison out, one thrust at a time.

She's got her back against the wall in the back room, legs parted like a prayer I'll never say. Her breath catches, a gasp sliced open by the way I drive into her.

It's hard, desperate, like this is the only goddamn thing keeping me from falling apart.

My cock buried deep, her moan catching fire in her throat, I chase oblivion in the slick heat of her, every stroke a fuck-you to the past and everything I swore I'd never become.

The desperation in her eyes tells me she's starving, fucking ravenous for more. She clings to me like I'm the last fix she'll ever get.

She doesn't know my name.

I don't know hers.

We're ghosts to each other, and that's the fucking point. Names come with strings, with expectations.

I'm not here for any of that shit. I'm here to fuck the rage out of me.

To shove the weight of my life into someone else's skin, just long enough to breathe again. To forget. To break apart and not have to put the pieces back together.

She's a body. Warm. Wet. Willing.

That's it. That's all.

She moans like I'm salvation, but I'm not. I'm the storm she's letting wreck her for a night, and when it's done, we'll both disappear into the smoke. As if it never fucking happened.

Because that's what this is. A fuck. A release.

Not a beginning. Just another end.

I slam into her, harder this time.

The brick grates against her back, but she doesn't complain. She just moans like this means something. Like I'm something.

I grit my teeth.

She doesn't get it.

This isn't about her.

Her hands claw at my back, nails scoring lines down my skin like she's trying to brand me.

I don't care. She could draw blood and I still wouldn't flinch. All I feel is the friction, the heat, the tightness around my cock as I drive into her again and again, chasing that edge like it's the only thing keeping me alive.

She whimpers something soft, breathy, too fucking much, and I want to tell her to shut the fuck up. I don't want her moans. I don't want her sounds.

I want silence. Stillness. Obedience.

She's just a hole tonight. A body. Warm, slick, and in the right place at the right fucking time. This isn't about her getting off. I'm not here to make her come.

I'm here to fuck the weight off my chest, to bury the shitstorm of my life inside someone else for five goddamn minutes and feel nothing.

My phone blares over the noise.

That ring tone I'd know anywhere. My father.

The man runs a mafia empire. When he calls, you answer.

No exceptions. No delays. Obedience is the currency.

But right now I couldn't give a fuck, when I'm buried balls-deep in some girl, fucking like my sanity depends on it. Because I'm not his soldier right now. I'm not his clean-up crew or his heir or his goddamn puppet.

Right now, I'm just a man with a cock and a reason to forget. I clench my jaw and fuck harder, like I can outrun the consequences.

"Don't fucking stop," she breathes against my ear, her voice all heat and hunger. Like she thinks she has a say in it. She fucking doesn't.

She can whisper, beg, fucking scream and I couldn't give a shit. I call the shots. I hold the reins.

I slam into her harder, faster.

Each thrust a fucking punishment, a purge, a desperate attempt to empty out the venom curling in my gut.

Her body jerks with every hit, trembling around me, trying to keep up with a rhythm that has nothing to do with pleasure and everything to do with pain. Her moans rise, broken, fucking relentless.

And all they do is drive me faster. Harder.

Closer to the edge I've been chasing since the second I shoved my cock inside her.

My grip tightens on her hips like I'm afraid she'll vanish mid-fuck.

It's coming. And I fucking welcome it.

That sharp, blinding rush that rips through me like a goddamn firestorm. My body locks, every muscle pulled tight as the release hits. Raw and violent and mine. A groan tears from my throat before I can swallow it, rough and guttural like it's been buried in me too long.

I come hard, hips grinding as I empty inside her, lost in the pleasure that sears through me and burns out the emptiness.

And for a breath, for a heartbeat, there's nothing but silence.

No noise.

No father.

No orders. No guilt.

When I'm done, I pull out as if she's nothing. No warning. No tenderness.

She gasps, reaching for me, fingers trembling as they grab at my arm as though she thinks I might stay. As if I ever would.

She doesn't get it. She's not special. Not different. Just another desperate girl hoping a good fuck might mean something more.

I tie off the condom, toss it in the trash, then tuck my cock back into my pants. Her scent still clings to me. I don't even glance at her while I zip up.

"That's it, sweetheart," I mutter, voice rough, dead cold. "Don't get fucking attached."

She flinches as if I've slapped her.

Pain's a better teacher than any lie I could've whispered in her ear.

I wipe my hands on my pants, brushing away the last trace of her like she's filth clinging to my skin... or dirt under my nails, nothing more.

My gaze shifts to hers for just a heartbeat. Her hair is messy, her lips swollen, and her pupils wide, as she still waits for something real.

I turn away from her without a second glance.

No parting words. No look back. She's already fading into the background, just another fuck I'll forget by morning.

The bass of the club thrums with the intensity of a second heartbeat, dirty and relentless, pulsing through the floors as I head to the door.

The real exit - the one the public never sees. The one my father made sure I had access to the second I was old enough to fuck and old enough to work for him.

A back door carved into the bones of the building, not for safety, but strategy. An escape route in case I ever got stuck. Trapped with a gun in my face, or my cock in someone I shouldn't have touched. Too young to give a shit. Too angry to care who it was with.

Salvatore's already there, my father's man, carved from silence and shadow, stationed like a ghost with a pulse.

He's seen it all.

The late-night fucks. The club girls who thought I might call. The blood on my knuckles when things got messy and I didn't stop swinging. He doesn't flinch. Doesn't speak. Doesn't ask questions he already knows the answers to.

He just gives me a nod, shoves the door open, and leads me out into the night as if it's routine... because it is. It's the same sins with a different girl.

The car's already waiting, blacked out and humming, as though it knows exactly what kind of wreck it's about to carry home.

The car door shuts behind me with a hollow thud, like a coffin lid sealing shut. The stench of sweat and sex still clings to me, thick in the air, but the silence in here feels worse.

The ringtone slices through the silence like a rusted blade.

Old, familiar, and still sharp enough to cut. That sound, I'd know it in my fucking sleep.

It's the anthem of control. A siren song wrapped in power plays and promises. It coils around my spine before I even move, dragging me back into the grip I've spent my whole life trying to outrun.

I reach into my pocket, my fingers wrapping around the phone as if it were something dirty.

His name flashes on the screen.

KING PRICK.

Bold, unblinking, like he's staring through me.

The vibration hums in my palm, steady as a threat.

I stare at it, jaw ticking.

One second.

Two.

Then I swipe it and hold it to my ear.

"What is it?" I growl, the words sharp, teeth bared, irritation bubbling like acid in my chest.

His voice slips through the speaker, clean, cold, and clinical. Always calm. Always in fucking control.

It crawls under my skin and lights a fire I've never learned how to put out. Because this phone... It's a fucking collar. And I've been wearing it since the day I was born.

"I found her," he says.

And everything inside me goes fucking still.

Those three words tear through me like shrapnel, tearing open shit I've spent years trying to bury. I never wanted to hear those words.

Not from him. Not from anyone. I've prayed. I've actually fucking prayed that she'd stay hidden. Stay gone. Stay safe.

Because if he ever found her... It's over.

The silence stretches, thick and strangling. My grip on the phone turns to stone, knuckles white as my throat locks.

"Get here, now," he says, voice steel, emotionless.

CHAPTER TWO

EMERY

The low hum of the fluorescent lights buzzes like it's trying to crawl inside my skull. The hiss of the griddle and the clatter of plates echo through the diner, filling the space as always.

Dinner rush.

If you can even call it that. More like a trickle of tired souls looking for something hot and salty to remind them they're still breathing. It's mostly truckers, lonely old men, and couples too tired to pretend they're still in love. Same faces. Same orders. Same shitty jokes.

But safe. The kind of safe that numbs your edges. The kind I've begged for.

Because boredom means no blood. No guns. No ghosts.

I scribble down a two-patty melt, extra onions, a side of fries, and a slice of that fake-ass cherry pie sitting in the front case like it hasn't been there for three days straight.

The order pad crinkles in my hand as I tear the slip free, passing it to Pete behind the counter without looking up.

My smile is automatic, tight, practiced, nothing more than muscle memory.

Then the bell above the door rings. Every part of me goes still. The kind that wraps around your spine akin to a noose. The kind that knows before your brain catches up that something's off.

My fingers curl against the counter. My breath stalls in my throat. I don't turn.

Not yet.

Because I already feel it.

That shift in the air. Because I know the past doesn't knock. It doesn't creep or whisper or ask permission. It kicks the fucking door down and walks in as if it never left.

When I finally glance over, I don't look directly at him. Just a flick of my eyes. A quick sweep. Casual. Cautious.

But it's enough.

He stands near the door as if he owns the room, or like he's deciding whether to burn it down. Posture relaxed but not slouched. Controlled. Calculated.

Mid-forties, maybe fifty. Salt cutting through his dark hair at the temples. Not soft, not tired... seasoned, as if life has tried to wear him down, but he hasn't let it win. His suit is dark and impeccable, not flashy but expensive, giving off the impression that he doesn't quite belong in this rundown diner, with its cracked vinyl booths and flickering lights.

He appears to be someone who doesn't have to ask for things twice. And that alone sets every nerve in my body on edge.

But it's not the suit.

Not the scar.

He carries a weight within him, similar to violence stitched beneath his skin.

It's the way he looks at me. Calm, direct, and too steady. It's as though I'm not a stranger. It's as if I'm not safe. He knows me. Not the me I've built here with lies and diner grease and a false name. The other me. The one I swore was dead and buried.

My hand tightens around the handle of the coffee pot as if I'm holding on for dear life. The plastic digs into my skin—unforgiving, cheap, and far too familiar. Just like everything else in this goddamn place. My knuckles go white, tendons straining as though they want to snap.

My heart doesn't just beat... it slams, a brutal thud-thud-thud against my ribs, like it's trying to punch its way out of my chest.

Every pulse is a scream I can't let out. Not here. Not now.

"You alright?" Pete asks, glancing over his shoulder, voice casual, he doesn't feel the fucking storm building in the room.

"Yeah."

It slips out like smoke. A lie wrapped in silk. Polished, practiced, poison.

I keep moving, pretending I don't see him. Pretending my skin isn't crawling or my past isn't whispering in my ear that it's finally caught up.

Because it's been years.

I changed my name. My life. My everything. Cut and colored my hair. Killed the girl I used to be and built someone new in her place.

But some nights, I still wake up sweating, my heart racing, convinced there's a shadow at the end of my bed. I still hear footsteps that aren't there, doors creaking open that never moved. I still brace myself every time I turn a corner, muscles tensed like a loaded gun, waiting for the worst.

Waiting to see him. Matteo, or his cold, fucked-up excuse for a father. Or worse... someone they sent for me. Someone resembling this. And tonight, it feels as if maybe that day finally showed the fuck up.

I avoid him like he's a loaded gun with the safety off.

No eye contact. No pass-by glances.

I stick to the opposite side of the diner as though the floor might burn if I step too close.

But he doesn't move. Doesn't speak. Just sits.

Silent.

Still.

Watching.

Like I'm not a waitress, but more as if I'm a fucking target.

Suzie, bless her oblivious heart, breezes over and pours him a cup of coffee like he's just another sad, lonely asshole killing time between bad decisions.

She doesn't feel the shift in the air. Doesn't see the way it coils tight around him. Around me.

But I do.

Every second he stays, my nerves fray thinner, and my skin crawls harder. I'm two seconds from tearing off my apron and getting the fuck out of here, heart in my throat, legs already halfway to the door... but then he stands and I watch him leave.

By the time my shift ends, I'm running on fumes and frayed nerves. Every fake smile, every order barked at me like I'm nothing, has scraped me raw.

I rip off my apron as if it's suffocating me, mutter a half-hearted goodbye no one hears, and shove open the back door.

The cold hits me with the force of a slap. It sinks into my bones. The streets are always dead this time of the night, and tonight is no different. I tuck my chin deeper into my coat, arms crossed tight over my chest, my makeshift armor, and force my legs to move.

The same sidewalk beneath my boots, the cracks etched into my memory with the permanence of scars I never asked for. The same alley seems to be watching me, waiting.

My heart kicks harder, a sudden jolt against my ribs like it's trying to warn me before my brain can catch up.

I tell myself it's nothing. Just the paranoia again. The ghosts I keep tucked under my skin making noise in the dark.

Then I hear it.

Footsteps.

Heavy.

Slow.

Deliberate. Gravel crunching beneath boots.

Each step echoing down the alley like a countdown I didn't know had started.

I don't think. I react. My body spins before my brain catches up, heart slamming against my ribs as if it's trying to claw its way out. My breath sticks in my throat, sharp and useless.

There's no time to scream.

No time to run.

A shadow spills from the dark, fast and close.

Something clamps over my mouth before the air can leave my lungs.

A rag, soaked in something sharp and chemical that burns the inside of my nose. My body jerks, fights, thrashes like instinct is trying to outrun inevitability, but it's already over. My limbs go heavy, and the world starts to tilt. The stars above me blur. The alley spins. My knees buckle. I hear my own breath, rough and useless against fabric.

Then nothing. Just the sound of the world slipping away.

The world returns in fragments.

Every inch of me is heavy, and numb. My head throbs, a slow, pulsing beat that feels like it's trying to crack open my skull from the inside. My eyelids flutter, but it's no use. Darkness presses in thick, smothering anything that might've passed for light.

My lungs seize. My chest tightens.

Panic wraps around my ribs, and I can't tell if it's from this place.

My arms are yanked behind me, wrists twisted in rope that bites deep, raw skin screaming with every twitch. There are metal chains wrapped around my waist that hold me tightly against the chair. Real ones. The kind meant to hold monsters or make you into one.

I shift and feel the cold edge of metal dig into my spine.

A chair. Heavy. Solid. Cruel. The kind meant to hold someone who isn't supposed to leave.

I try to move. Fight. Strain. But my body won't play along.

It aches in places I can't name. A dull, deep kind of pain, layered beneath the sharper ones. My limbs are lead, every joint locked up in protest, every movement answered by agony.

Whatever the hell they gave me is still in my system. My head spins every time I blink. The room tilts even though I can't see it.

But even in the dark, even through the fog in my brain, I feel him. That cold weight in the air. That familiar static crawling over my skin.

Matteo.

The name slams through me like a punch to the gut.

Because I know without even seeing, without hearing, without proof of him standing in front of me, I know this has his fingerprints all over it.

I feel him.

That same suffocating presence that coils around my ribs as if it were wire, squeezes the breath from my lungs as punishment. A reminder.

Every breath. Every step.

I'm right back in it. The world I ran from. The name I shed like skin. The life I clawed my way out of, bloodied and broken, just to taste freedom for the first time in years. Now I'm back in the grip of the man I swore I'd never face again. Back in the goddamn fire, choking on smoke I thought I'd finally outrun.

A bulb snaps on with a click, and the light punches through my eyelids like a fucking spotlight. It's harsh. Yellow and unforgiving. It's the kind of light that doesn't reveal, it exposes.

My eyes squint against it, twitching, refusing to cooperate. Everything in me wants to stay under, to sink back into the dark I was drowning in. But the brightness keeps clawing at me, dragging me up by the throat.

Muscles slow. Vision blurred. Every blink is a losing battle.

I force my eyes open slowly, lashes sticking together like they've been glued shut by the dark. Light burns at the edges, and the world tilts sideways as my lashes lift, slow and shaking. The edges of reality smudged with shadows and pain.

Then I see him.

A silhouette carved out by the light, standing dead in front of me. Shoulders squared, posture locked with that rigid, quiet control I could never forget. His face is swallowed by shadow, but it doesn't matter. The shape of him hits like a punch to the chest. Broad frame. Sharp edges. His presence is a fucking weapon.

My stomach knots, tight and mean, a sick twist of panic and knowing. Because I know exactly who the fuck is standing there. And I know exactly how fucked I am.

And for a split second... just one—I panic.

Not because he's here. But because of what I've got stashed away.

The files. The ones that could bring everything crashing down if he ever found out. If this is about that... if he knows... No. He can't. He can't know.

This man staring me down isn't the boy I once loved.

That boy had softness behind his eyes, heat in his hands, and a future hidden in his grin. This one... He's colder now. Sharper. Like the world carved the softness out of him and left nothing behind but steel and silence.

I jerk against the restraints again, harder this time, metal clanging with a warning bell no one's going to answer. The rope bites deep into my wrists, the pain sharp, but it's still better than doing nothing. Better than sitting still while he watches me in a way that I'm prey that wandered back into his trap.

I grit my teeth and pull again.

That's when his voice cuts through the silence.

"Stop fucking moving," he snaps, the words cold and razor clean. "You'll only make it worse."

He steps forward, slow and lethal, like every inch of him is wound tight with purpose. The light finally catches his face. It's sharper than I remember, harder.

His eyes don't flicker. They don't soften.

They just look at me like I'm the problem he's already solved.

"You think you can fight this? Fight me," His mouth curls, but it's not a smile. It's a warning dressed up in cruelty. "Go ahead. Keep struggling. Maybe if you bleed enough, you'll finally remember who the fuck you're dealing with."

My breath stutters, catching in my chest before I can stop it. But I recover quickly, lifting my chin slowly, ignoring the burn in my wrists because the fury pulsing beneath my skin is louder, stronger, more fucking real.

Matteo has always said it, even when we were kids, whispered with the reverence of gospel into my ear, "Never let your enemy know you're scared."

Now he's the enemy.

Now he's the one standing across from me, with cold eyes and an even colder heart, trying to carve fear from my flesh.

So, I do exactly what he taught me. I stare back at him, bury every tremor behind a steady gaze and razor smile, and speak low, cold, cutting—

"Still pretending you're in control, Matteo? Is that cute little monster act working for you these days?"

His jaw tightens, just barely, but I fucking see it.

I lean in as far as the ropes and chains will let me, eyes locked on his.

My voice drops to a whisper, sharp as broken glass.

"Deep down, you're still the same fucked-up little boy playing dress-up in daddy's suit, aren't you?" I let it sit there. Let it burn for a moment before I speak again. "You don't scare me. Not because you've changed... but because you haven't."

He takes a step and the light catches on that smirk, crooked, and cruel, and yet so damn familiar it hits like a punch to the ribs.

He steps even closer, still with that smirk tugging at his mouth, it's smug, dangerous. But underneath the cruelty, for the briefest second, I see it, it's him. The boy who once held my heart as if it wasn't a weapon. The boy who used to whisper promises instead of threats.

"You think a few years, a new name, and some fucked-up sense of pride makes you dangerous?" He leans in. "You were better when you were begging."

I smile, all teeth. "You were better when you had a soul."

He laughs. It's cold and sharp. "You think you ever touched my soul, sweetheart?" He tilts his head, voice hardening. "You were a fuck. A habit I broke. Nothing more."

"Still pretending you're untouchable, Matteo?" I breathe. "I've seen you on your knees, remember... Whispering that you loved me as though it was the last fucking truth in the world."

And then his smirk comes, crueler than before.

"You think I'll turn back into that pathetic bastard who thought he could save you. Who used to love fucking you like it meant something."

His hand yanks the chain tight, dragging me closer. The chair jerks beneath me.

"You think this is about love?" he growls. "This is fucking war, Em. And you're on the losing side of it."

I don't flinch. I lean in as if I want to taste blood.

"I was never on your side, Matteo," I spit, voice cold as the grave he left me in. "Not after you left me bleeding as if I was nothing."

The chain clinks as he steps back, letting it fall between us like a line drawn in blood. The smirk slips from his face, replaced with something sharper, deadly cold, and certain.

"We're done playing," he says, voice low and flat, reminiscent of a man used to giving orders before pulling the trigger. "Next time you open that smart little mouth of yours, I won't just shut it up. I'll drag a knife across your throat so slow you'll feel every fucking inch of it. I'll carve my name so deep into your fucking skin while you bleed out at my feet, so when you take your last breath, you'll remember exactly who did this to you."

His stare lingers... long enough to burn, long enough to brand, and then he turns, walking away like I'm already dead. Like I was never more than a loose end waiting to be tied off.

The door shuts behind him, a vault sealing tightly and locking away everything we will never say.

I swallow the fear down, force my spine straight, and let the anger rise to meet it.

Because if this is war... He better be ready to bleed for it. Because I'll burn everything down before I let him win.

Chapter Three

Matteo

I turn from the door and lock my eyes on her through the one-way glass.

Emery. Or Emma, now.

That bullshit alias painted over her as a disguise that could never hide what she really is. A fake name and a hair color that doesn't fucking suit her. It's too soft, too quiet. As if she's trying to erase the fire that used to burn beneath it.

But I see through all of it.

Head held high. Spine straight.

Eyes sharp enough to cut clean through glass, and fuck, they almost do.

She's still got that fire in her gaze, the same one that used to light me up from the inside out and burn everything else to ash. She's sitting there as if she's daring the world to break her.

Or daring me too.

And the fucked-up part... I don't know if I want to tear her down or fall to my knees and beg her to forgive me for what comes next.

There's blood on her wrists. Rage in her eyes. She's bruised and bound to a chair built to break her, and still... still she doesn't fucking flinch. She doesn't look down. Doesn't give me a single crack to crawl into. She radiates strength like it's stitched into her goddamn bones.

She's still got it. That thing that slides under my skin with the sensation of barbed wire. Twisted in deep, impossible to rip out without tearing muscle. That thing that's been in me since the first time she looked at me as if I wasn't just a cocky son of a bitch with blood on his hands.

She's still beautiful. Fuck, she's beautiful. Even now.

That face. The same one I used to cradle between my hands like it was the only soft thing this fucked-up world ever gave me. Those lips... fuck, those lips that I used to lose myself in, imagining that if I kissed her long enough, all the hard parts of me would finally break away.

She's still her. Still, the girl I burned for. Still, the girl who knew how to cut through every mask I wore and drove her fucking fingers into the heart I swore I didn't have.

And now how the fuck am I supposed to break her.

But that's the job. There's no room for hesitation. My father made it clear that she knows something. And now it's on me to rip it out of her, piece by fucking piece. Strip her down, break her open, drag the truth from her lips no matter how hard she fights. Crush what's left of that fire until all that's left is ash and the truth.

My phone buzzes in my pocket. It's short, sharp, and demanding.

Of fucking course it's Him.

He's checking in, expecting the job to be done already, expecting her broken and bleeding truth at my feet.

I let it ring once more. Breathe in, like it'll settle the shit unraveling in my chest.

It doesn't.

I press the phone to my ear. "Yeah."

"Status."

No warmth.

No patience.

Just that clipped, surgical tone that always says more than the words do. My father doesn't ask questions, he issues expectations.

"She's here," I say, jaw tight.

A pause. Not hesitation. Just pressure. The kind that builds behind your ribs and waits to snap.

"And the information?"

Like it should've already been spilled. Breaking her should've been as easy as flipping a switch.

"Nothing yet."

"You're dragging your feet."

I grit my teeth. "I'm working her."

"She's here to be emptied, Matteo. I don't give a shit that she was your childhood friend, or whatever the fuck she meant to you back then. None of that matters. You get the information, names, codes, everything. Rip it out of her, fuck it out of her if you have to. Just get it done."

My hand tightens around the phone. "I said I've got it."

"Then fucking act like it. If you can't get the information, I'll get someone who can."

The line goes dead.

No warning. No second chances.

Just a command dressed like a threat, and silence that sounds eerily similar to I'm replaceable.

I slide the phone back into my pocket, jaw clenched so tight it fucking aches.

His words still echo in my head, cold, final, unforgiving. *"Rip it out of her. Fuck it out of her if you have to."*

I swallow the disgust rising in my throat.

Not at the order.

At how easy it would be. To fall back into that again.

To fuck her and make it mean something. To bury everything between us in sweat and skin. To pretend I'm not giving him exactly what he wants—and feeding the sick part of me that still fucking craves her.

I turn back to the glass. She's sitting like a queen on a fucking throne, wrists raw, jaw locked, as though the ropes and chains don't mean shit. As if she's not the one trapped here.

She lifts her head, slow and unbothered, and stares straight at the glass, right through it, as though she knows I'm there. She's daring me to walk in and try again.

She thinks she can outlast me. Outplay me. This is still some fucked-up echo of who we used to be.

Fuck this, it's time to go in. Time to finish this shit. If she doesn't want to talk... Then I'll break her until she does.

The door swings open.

She doesn't blink. Doesn't flinch. Her eyes lock on mine the second I step through, as though she's been waiting just to piss me off.

I walk in slowly. Every step is deliberate. Heavy. Controlled. The kind of quiet that comes before something violent.

She tilts her head, mouth curling into that smug, smartass smirk I used to taste in the dark.

"I thought they'd send the muscle in," she says, sweet as fucking poison. "After Daddy's little boy couldn't get the job done."

I stop in front of her, and for half a second, the room is nothing but heat. Pressure. Her mouth and that fucking voice, crawling under my skin like she's still got the right to be there.

I stare her down.

"You'll bleed, Em. You'll scream. And when you finally beg, it won't be for mercy… it'll be for me to fucking end it."

She laughs. Low. Bitter. Reminiscent of something jagged being dragged across bone.

"Careful," she says, voice colder than ice. "If watching me bleed gets your cock hard, Matteo, maybe you're already the monster he always wanted you to be." Her eyes gleam with venom. "Or maybe that's the point. Maybe Daddy didn't turn you into a monster. Maybe you always were one, just waiting for his permission."

Her eyes lock on mine, unshaken, burning.

Something inside me snaps.

I lunge forward, grab a fistful of her hair, and yank her head back hard. Forcing her face up, right where I want it.

Her breath catches, but she doesn't look away. Doesn't fucking blink.

She's defiant right to the end.

Good.

Let her fight me with that fire. I'll rip it out of her with my bare hands.

"You want to fuck me up?" she hisses. "Do it, Matteo. Break my bones. Rip me open if you have to. But don't kid yourself… this isn't about information."

"You think this is a fucking game? That I give a fuck about you?" I snarl, my face inches from hers, my grip tight enough to make her scalp burn. "Keep talking, Em. Keep running that pretty little mouth. Every word out of it just makes me want to ruin you more."

I tighten my hold, yanking her head back until her neck strains, forcing her to meet my eyes.

"You're not in control here. You don't get to laugh, or smirk, or talk about who I am or what we were." My voice is razor sharp. Merciless. "You are nothing. Never were. Just some hole I used to practice on. Just soft skin and noise while I figured out how to fuck."

I watch her face, waiting for the reaction, the rage, the hurt, anything. But I'm not finished.

My voice drops, low, a quiet kind of cruelty.

"If you died in this chair tonight, no one would give a fuck. Not even me. I'd walk out of here, clean my hands, and sleep like a fucking baby."

I hold her face exactly where I want it, hard, ruthless, waiting for her to break.

She just stares right back, those eyes of hers burning holes through my fucking soul. And my traitorous gaze slips down, just for a second, landing on those lips. The same lips I spent years trying to forget.

Fuck. I try not to notice them, try not to think how easy it'd be to lean in just a little further, close the distance between us and see if they still taste the same. If they're still as soft, still as perfect as I remember. If she'd still gasp the way she used to when I took her mouth like I owned it.

She sees it.

That one second my eyes dropped to her mouth. That moment I let the past crawl back in through a fucking crack.

And she smirks as though she's already won. It's slow. Knowing, and fucking infuriating.

"Aww," she says, voice low, "is this the part where you pretend you don't want to kiss me?"

Her smile widens like she's already won.

I laugh. Just once. Low and cold, the sound scraping out of my throat.

"You think I'd kiss that mouth of yours?" I murmur, dragging my gaze down to that smart little mouth she can't seem to fucking shut. "Sweetheart, if I touched it again, it wouldn't be for kissing. It'd be with your lips wrapped around my cock. Not because you want it, because I fucking own it. Just like every other fucking part of you."

She draws in a sharp breath, but I don't let her speak.

I lean in, close enough that she can feel every filthy word hit her skin.

"You want to talk control, Em?" My voice drops, pure threat. "Keep running that mouth, and I'll fuck the words right out of your throat."

She's silent. Not afraid. Not broken. She's just defiant.

It's in her eyes… the way she looks at me in a manner suggesting she's still got the upper hand. No matter what I say, or what I threaten her with, I'll never truly reach her.

My fingers twist into her hair and I yank. Harder this time, just enough to bend her neck, to force her spine into something rigid.

Her throat is exposed and fuck, I want to look. I want to stare at it. Trace the lines with my eyes the way I used to trace them with my mouth. I want to remember how soft it felt under my lips. How she used to tilt her head back not from fear, but from fucking need.

"Where's your father?" I ask, voice cold, controlled, but shaking at the edges.

She doesn't answer.

Of course, she fucking doesn't.

I lean in, lips near her ear, voice barely more than a breath. "You think I won't fucking hurt you?" I murmur. "You think I won't become exactly what he made me?" I pull back and force her to meet my eyes. "Because I will, Em. I'll fucking become him if I have to." I stare at her like I don't remember who she used to be. As if I haven't dreamed about her every night since she vanished. "Answer me," I snarl. "This is me choosing not to ruin you."

Her eyes blaze. Just that raw, untamed defiance I used to worship. Now it mocks me. Taunts me like a dare. And then she spits it, the words tearing from her throat with the intensity of something that's been waiting there, soaking in gasoline.

"I don't fucking know."

"You do fucking know," I growl, the words dragged from somewhere deep. "Don't play dumb with me, Em. Not now."

Her mouth twitches. No smirk this time. Just fury.

"I don't know, Matteo," she snaps, eyes wild with fire.

I don't believe her. I can't. Because if she's telling the truth, then I've got nothing left but violence or failure. So I let the anger take over.

I shove her back in the chair harder. Hard enough so she feels it in her spine. Hard enough to make the chains bite into her skin.

"You're lying," I say, standing over her like a shadow she can't outrun. "Say it again. Look me in the eye and fucking say it."

She glares up at me, chest heaving.

"I. Don't. Fucking. Know."

Each word hits as a punch to the ribs. Because I want them to be a lie. I fucking need them to be a lie. Because if they're not... Then I'm not getting the information my father needs. I'm not doing my job extracting the information from her. Because if she's telling the truth... Then I'll be hurting her for nothing.

And if I stop now. If I don't break her, my father will send someone who won't hesitate. Someone who won't care what she was to me.

I stand there, staring down at her as if she's the fucking trigger and I'm the loaded gun. My breath is ragged, fists tight, as though if I don't do something, I'll come apart right here in front of her.

"Who's protecting him, Em?" My voice is low, lethal, meant to wound.

Her eyes narrow, defiance crackling behind them.

"Who's hiding the bastard that sold you out?" I press, each word like a shove.

She jerks against the cuffs, teeth bared, snarling as if feral. "My father would never sell out his family," she yells. "He's nothing fucking close to you."

I laugh, sharp and cruel. "He already fucking did, Em."

"No," she spits. "Don't stand there acting like you're better than him as if you're some righteous fucking executioner. You take orders from the same monster that built him. You became what he tried to protect me from."

"He sold you out," I say, eyes locked on hers, daring her to deny it. "Traded you. He fucking pawned you off to the highest bidder and didn't look back." I pause, letting the silence rot between us. "He gave you up to save himself. And you're still bleeding loyalty for a man who never even flinched."

"I don't believe you," she says.

"How the fuck do you think I found you, Em?" I snap. "My father was the highest bidder."

She freezes. Not all at once. Just a flicker. A blink. A breath that catches in her throat.

But I see it.

The crack. The mask slips just enough for the pain to crawl through. The kind of pain that doesn't scream, it just sinks in.

I should feel satisfied. I should press harder. But instead, something shifts in my chest.

Because for the first time since I walked into this room, she falters. And for a breath, just one, I see the girl I used to protect. The one I swore I'd never let anyone break her like this.

Her lips part like she wants to fight, but the words don't come.

Just the silence. Just the fucking hurt staring back at me through eyes that used to look at me as if I was hers.

My grip on her hair loosens. Not all the way, just enough for her to breathe again. Enough for my fingers to stop trembling from how close I'd come to pushing her past the edge.

She's quiet now. Eyes glassy, lips parted, that sharp tongue of hers swallowed by the kind of heartbreak that steals your breath and never gives it back.

And fuck, I hate it. Hate myself for putting it there.

But before I can move, before I can say anything, the door behind me creaks open.

Then the sound of boots on concrete.

I release my grip on her hair and turn.

Rocco.

One of my father's men. Leather gloves. Black jacket. Dead eyes. He's the kind of man who doesn't ask questions, just follows orders. The cleanup crew. The final nail.

His gaze skims past me to her. It's cold, calculated. Like he's already sizing up how many pieces she'll break into when it's his turn to do what I couldn't.

"What the fuck are you doing here?" I snap, my voice dropping into something just a breath from violence.

His presence, it's a fucking threat. A loaded gun pointed at both of us, disguised in leather and silence.

Rocco's eyes shift to mine, slow and empty. "Boss said to check if she's still breathing," He says, voice flat. "Said if you weren't making progress, maybe someone else should."

His gaze cuts to her one final time, and fuck, that's all it takes. Something detonates inside me, brutal and blinding, like a bomb going off behind my ribs. A rupture I can't contain, it's wide enough to burn through every ounce of control I thought I had.

Then Rocco speaks.

"You might want to call your father," he says. "I've been given clearance. I'm the one extracting the information now."

The words hit harder than any bullet I've ever taken.

I've been given clearance.

He's not asking. He's informing me. Like I'm already obsolete. As if I'm just a ghost in this fucking room while he puts his hands on her.

He moves around me. I'm not a threat anymore. I've already been dismissed, discarded without a second thought, like I never fucking mattered.

My gaze follows him, every muscle coiled tight, every breath thick with the taste of blood I haven't spilled yet.

"Touch her," I say, voice dropping into something darker. "And I'll bury you so fucking deep even my father won't find you."

He pauses.

It's just for a second, but enough for me to see the flicker in his eyes.

I know this man. I've seen what he's capable of.

The cruelty. The way he breaks people. Beats them to a pulp until they can't see through their own blood, can't talk through the teeth he's forced them to swallow.

He's stepping into a firestorm. And if he fucking touches her... if he even thinks about laying a hand on her... I'll burn him alive. I'll make sure his blood stains these walls, and I won't stop until the screams I hear are his.

Rocco doesn't flinch. His dead, soulless eyes scan me.

"You think I'm here to listen to your threats, Matteo?" he sneers, voice flat, dripping with that sickening condescension. "Call your father. Let him know you couldn't get the job done."

My blood fucking boils.

Rocco steps closer to her. His eyes flicker over her like she's something to claim, something to break. He grabs her hair, pulling her head back to expose her throat. His fingers dig in, and he yanks her head back further, just enough to make her feel every inch of his dominance.

"Maybe I should fuck it out of you instead," he mutters, voice dripping with cruel amusement, the words slithering through the air like venom. "See how fast I can break you."

Emery's gaze doesn't waver. She doesn't flinch, doesn't cower. Her eyes burn with a fierce, unbroken defiance. The fire that's always been there doesn't die, it just flares even brighter.

She chuckles. It's low and bitter, her lips curling into a smirk.

"Yeah, sure. Do you think your tiny cock's gonna make me talk? Please," she retorts.

Rocco's eyes burn with rage, and I can see it. The insult lands. Hard. The muscle in his neck twitches, and his fist curls. I watch him, waiting, because I know exactly what's coming.

She's pushing all his buttons, with that mouth that's still running. But fuck, she has no idea of who or what she's playing with.

Rocco jerks his arm back, fist ready to smash into her.

The rage burns hotter than anything I've ever felt, black and searing, tearing through every part of me. I can feel it crawling under my skin, dragging me further down into the abyss. It's not just anger anymore; it's an urge to destroy.

My hand moves without thinking, reaching into my jacket, fingers curling around the cold metal of the gun. The weight of it steadies me. Feels familiar. Feels like it belongs.

I don't think. I don't hesitate. I step forward, with no words, just cold, brutal action.

The gun clicks into place. I line it up with the back of Rocco's head.

One shot. One clean fucking shot.

I pull the trigger.

CHAPTER FOUR

EMERY

The deafening crack of the gunshot rips through the air. A brutal explosion that shatters the silence. It echoes through my chest and causes every muscle to seize up, my heart pounding against my ribs like it's trying to claw its way out.

The shock hits first, and for a moment, I can't breathe. I'm drowning in it.

The weight of the noise. The impact that settles into my bones. It vibrates in my skull, a fucking war drum pounding through every nerve. But what hits next isn't just the deafening noise.

It's the blood. The warm, slick spray that coats my face. Each drop is a brutal reminder that mercy doesn't exist here anymore. It's a cruel fucking truth.

The liquid coats my skin, crawling over my face, slick and heavy, like it's been carved into me. The taste floods my senses, metallic, suffocating. Choking me from the inside out. I don't flinch.

I can't. I'm trapped, bound to this goddamn chair, my body screaming for escape, but every breath locks tighter around my ribs, a prison I'll never crawl free from.

Slowly, my eyes flutter open. Lashes stuck together with blood. The world blurs for a moment. Everything smeared in red and shock, and then... I see him.

Matteo.

He stands still, the weight of the world carving him into stone. His arm is outstretched, gun in hand, an extension of his body, of who he's become. The only thing that defines him now.

His expression is unreadable, cold as ice. Rocco's body lies crumpled at our feet, a broken shell of what he once was. The blood pools around him, dark and relentless, flowing like rivers of death, staining everything it touches, soaking into the very floor beneath us.

Matteo's eyes snap to mine, slamming into me with the force of a goddamn storm. They're wild, relentless, and for a split second, I wonder if this is it. If my name's already inked in blood, carved beside Rocco's, another body claimed by this fucked-up game.

A tremor rattles my chest. Panic crawls up my throat, bitter and burning, but I choke it down. I won't give him the satisfaction of seeing the fear tearing through me. If he's going to put a bullet in my head, then he can damn well look me in the fucking eyes when he does it.

I don't blink.

My eyes stay on him, jaw clenched tight, forcing myself to meet his gaze. I'm fighting to take control, even though he's got all the power. I'll be damned if he gets to see the terror that's eating me alive from the inside out.

Every second drags on, stretching out... suffocating me from the inside. My heart is racing, pulse hammering in my ears, drowning out everything else.

Then, after what feels like a lifetime, Matteo lowers the gun. I watch as he slides it back into his jacket pocket, the threat still hanging in the air, a flicker of a promise that he could pull it out again whenever the hell he wants.

He's not going to kill me.

Not today.

At least not yet.

He moves with the quiet precision of a man who's seen the worst of everything, like the violence he's just unleashed, Rocco's lifeless body on the floor, is nothing more than another item on his to-do list.

I don't dare look at him as he circles behind me, but I feel his eyes crawling over every inch of my skin, dissecting me piece by piece.

I only flinch when I feel his fingers graze the ropes binding my wrists. It's a soft touch... too soft, too fucking calm. His heat closes in, heavy against my skin, his presence thick enough to choke on. As he leans in to untie the knots, his breath brushes against my ear, sending a jolt straight through me. I stiffen, trying to force my body to stay still, but it's a losing fight. Fuck him, and my traitorous skin.

My heart hammers in my chest, so loud I'm sure he can hear it. His fingers move with clinical precision, loosening the ropes, but I can't focus on that. I can't focus on anything but the way his presence engulfs me, how I can't breathe without feeling him there. It's all too close, too real. Every inch of me screams to escape, but I can't. I'm fucking paralyzed by the intensity of him.

The ropes fall away with a soft snap, and I exhale a breath I didn't realize I was holding. My arms tremble. Bloodied wrists throb, shredded and raw, pain pulsing through every nerve. The burn in my shoulders still gnaws at me, a relentless reminder of how long I've been trapped, how long I've been nothing but a fucking prisoner to this chair.

The chains come next, their cold bite digging into my waist, a cruel reminder of how much power he's had over me. But it's not the metal that makes everything inside me twist. It's the way his fingers skim over my skin, savoring every second. Each touch sends a jolt through me, and I hate myself for how it makes my pulse race.

His touch triggers a tremor I can't suppress, even as every part of me screams to move, to pull away. But I don't. I won't. Not when his hands linger—owning me, staking claim to every inch of my skin.

The chains fall to the ground with a hollow clink, and the sound feels like it echoes through my bones.

Matteo steps back in front of me. His eyes lock onto mine, unflinching, unblinking, as if nothing and no one can ever break that cold, calculating gaze. Every inch of him screams control.

"You try to run," he growls. "I'll put a fucking bullet in your skull. No warning. No second chance."

His words don't just hit. They crash through me, a sledgehammer shattering glass. He's not here to play. Doesn't give a damn about what we were. There's no trace of the love we shared in his voice—only cold steel. No mercy. No deals. No bargains. His voice is a wall, an unyielding line in the sand that won't bend or break. Just another part of him that's turned to stone.

"Remember who decides whether you live or die," he says, voice cold as ice. "You think you can take one step without my permission?" He steps closer, his gaze searing into mine. "I'll put a bullet in your head before your feet even hit the fucking ground. Understand?"

I stay silent. The words sit there, trapped behind my teeth. But I keep them buried... because speaking them right now might just get me killed.

His eyes narrow, cold fire igniting behind them, a smoldering fury simmering just below the surface, ready to explode. His hand twitches toward the gun. It's not just the weight of the weapon, it's the unspoken promise that things could spiral from bad to catastrophic in the blink of an eye.

"Fucking tell me you understand, Emery."

It's not a request. It's not even a threat anymore. It's a fucking command. I see the muscles in his jaw twitch, the fury rising in his eyes, hot and dangerous, like I'm staring into the eye of a storm that could rip everything apart in seconds.

Then, his voice drops and I hear the threat. "Don't fuck around with me, Emery."

"I understand," I say. It's all I can give him. No pride left to hold onto. No room for defiance, no strength to argue.

Without a word, Matteo's hand closes around my arm. He jerks me forward, dragging me across the room with such force that I stumble, my feet barely scraping the floor.

The raw power in his touch leaves no room for resistance. My body's a toy in his hands, my movements not my own. He pulls me like I'm a ragdoll, his strength eclipsing any trace of control I could ever hope to hold.

Every step is a reminder that I am nothing. That I have no power in this situation.

When we reach the door he stops, just shy of the threshold. His body goes still, like he's waiting for something, watching for any threat that might slip through the cracks.

His hand moves to his jacket, pulling out the gun with a calm that makes the hairs on the back of my neck stand up.

He releases my arm, then curls his hand around the door handle and twists... slow, deliberate, like he's savoring the silence before the storm.

Matteo cracks the door open just enough to slide his gaze through. His eyes slicing through the shadows, searching every inch of the hallway like a predator waiting to pounce. There's no urgency, just cold calculation. A mind working through every possible threat lurking in the dark.

His eyes flick back to me. It's brief, but loaded, as if he's deciding whether I'm a threat worth crushing or just another pawn to bend beneath his control.

Then he grabs my arm again, yanking me forward with that same brutal, unflinching precision. Not a person. Just a thing to be handled, something to be dragged into line.

Then he steps through the open doorway, planting himself in front of me. A shield I didn't ask for but suddenly fucking need.

"Move," he growls, his voice low. And in this moment, I know that disobeying him is not an option.

The dim light flickers above us, stuttering like a dying heartbeat, casting jagged shadows that crawl across the walls and chase us down the hallway. Every flicker feels like a warning. A pulse of tension that crawls up my spine and coils at the base of my neck.

Matteo's grip on my arm tightens, forcing me to match his pace. Every step in sync with his.

He doesn't break stride as he moves toward the main entrance door. He throws me a quick glance, then drives his shoulder into the door. Shoving it open with one smooth, brutal motion, like it costs him nothing to tear through whatever's in his way.

The gun stays clenched in his hand, steady and sure, while his body moves with that lethal kind of grace. He's the calm in the eye of the storm. Dangerous as hell, untouchable, and dripping with authority that dares anyone to test him.

His eyes sweep the shadows. Every muscle drawn tight, wired to explode with the slightest trigger.

He doesn't move. Doesn't make a sound.

He just stands there, waiting, the night itself a threat. His gaze drags the area, taking everything in. There's a lethal kind of focus in his eyes, the kind that says he's already chosen what he'll destroy if shit goes sideways.

He stands still for a beat, every muscle coiled, like a predator testing the air for threats. He's not just scanning the dark, he's challenging it. Daring whatever's out there to come closer, to try him.

When he's convinced we're clear, he steps into the night, dragging me with him. The cold snaps against my skin. It's sharp and punishing, but Matteo doesn't twitch. His eyes are locked on the black car buried in the shadows. It's the only thing that exists, the only thing that matters in this fucked-up world we're walking back into.

I'm still in my thin work shirt, the cold digging in with claws, burying itself deep. I don't even know where my jacket went, the one I was wearing when I left the diner.

Matteo doesn't slow... not for the cold, not for me. His pace is relentless, eating up the distance until we're at the black car in seconds. He wrenches the passenger door open without a word, like patience was never part of the plan.

"Get your fucking ass in," he commands, his voice cold with cruelty.

He doesn't even look at me... just stands there, a mess he's been forced to clean up. His eyes are hollow, dead, every part of him that used to feel stripped away. Rigid posture. Clenched jaw. A man who gave up pretending to give a damn a long time ago.

And me... I'm just collateral damage. A problem he wants to erase, not fix.

I don't hesitate. I slide into the seat, and the door slams shut behind me with a heavy thud. A lock clicks into place. Whatever this is, there's no turning back now.

The silence that follows is deafening. Before I can even catch my breath, Matteo rounds the front of the car, expecting a ghost to drag itself out of the shadows. Every part of him wired for betrayal, convinced this is a setup.

He slides into the driver's seat with that same lethal calm, like he's done this a hundred times... with enemies, with ghosts, with girls who made the mistake of trusting him.

The door slams shut behind him. The gun rests on his thigh, casual as fuck, an extension of him. It doesn't need to be pointed at me to make a statement. It already is.

The engine growls to life, low and pissed off, as if it knows exactly where we're headed... and it's nowhere good. Headlights carve through the dark, cutting a path straight to fucking hell. His hands grip the wheel tight, knuckles white, jaw clenched—holding back a scream or the urge to kill. Rage rolls off him in thick, choking waves. He doesn't say a word. He doesn't have to. His silence screams louder than anything else ever could.

The car jerks forward, tires spitting against cracked asphalt, trying to shake the night off its back.

And just like that... we're gone.

Matteo drives as if we're being hunted, the past gnawing at his heels and survival riding on outrunning the devil with a fucking death wish. Every mile's a challenge. Every turn, a dare.

The silence between us is a pressure cooker... hissing, pulsing, toxic as fuck. It dares me to speak. Dares him to snap. But neither of us flinch. Not yet.

The engine screams as Matteo's foot slams harder on the gas, the car surging forward, fueled by rage. Black metal devours the road, slicing through the night, a blade tearing everything in its path. Shadows flicker past the windows, ghosts we leave behind.

But inside... it's just him and me. Trapped in a silence that roars louder than any fight.

Finally, I snap. The silence cuts too deep, coils too tight. My voice slices through it, jagged and raw.

"Where the fuck are we going?"

It's not a question, it's a challenge. Because sitting in this car with him, with that goddamn gun and all this unfinished shit between us, feels like waiting for a bomb to go off.

He doesn't even look at me, just keeps his eyes locked on the road with that lethal focus. But I see it. The twitch in his jaw, the way his fingers strangle the wheel, as if it's the only thing keeping him from snapping. He doesn't answer, but his silence... it fucking screams.

The heat climbs, curling in my chest, a flame I can't put out. But I don't back down. I lean into it.

"Answer me, Matteo." My voice is sharper now, cutting through the roar of the engine. "Where the fuck are we going?"

"Shut the fuck up, Em," he says, his gaze never leaving the road. "You don't get to ask questions. You don't get to know. You just fucking follow." His words hit like bullets. "You'll know when you need to know."

"God, you're such an asshole," I snap. "What is this... the fucking Matteo Show?" I hurl the words, each one sharper than the last. "I'm just supposed to sit here, all quiet and obedient while you play mafia king and expect me to be grateful I'm choking on your overpriced cologne. Fuck you, Matteo."

I wait.

For a twitch, a glance, a curse. For something.

But he gives me nothing. Not a flicker of interest. Not a goddamn blink. Like I'm just background noise he's learned to ignore.

So, I go for the one thing I know that used to hurt him the deepest, without ever spilling blood. I turn away from him. As if I'm bored. As if he's nothing. As if the fire between us never even scorched me.

And in the silence, I feel it.

A shift in him so slight it could be missed, but I don't. A small crack in his armor. Barely there. But still, it's enough. And for a second, it feels like a win.

I exhale hard, frustration burning in my chest as I rest my head against the cold glass. I won't look at him. I can't. Not at that stupid, gorgeous, maddening face. The one that makes me want to scream, cry, break something... or kiss him so hard I forget every reason as to why I should hate him.

The city outside blurs past. A smear of lights and shadows, slipping by too fast to hold onto, vanishing too fast to catch. My thoughts aren't any better. Broken. Feral. Caught in a loop that won't fucking let go.

Your father sold you out. Sold you like a fucking pawn to the highest bidder.

The thought of my own father, the man who was supposed to protect me, trading me as if I were nothing more than currency. It makes my stomach twist, bile rising under the weight of it. The betrayal burns, sinking its teeth in.

I was never his daughter. Just a debt to settle. A pawn shoved across the board by the one person who was supposed to fight for me.

And the worst part.... Some fucked-up part of me still wants to believe he didn't do it.

CHAPTER FIVE

MATTEO

The world outside is a blur of dark roads and distant lights. The silence finally doesn't feel suffocating.

Maybe it's because Emery's finally quiet, her smart mouth giving me a break for once. She's been sleeping for the past hour, her head resting against the seat, her body curled slightly, as if she's trying to shrink away from everything.

I glance at her, and it's hard not to notice how different she looks when she's not fighting. Her face is softer now, almost peaceful. She doesn't seem to be the same woman who challenged me at every turn, who fought me with every word.. But even in sleep, there's tension in her face, the kind that says her mind never fully lets go.

I can't help but watch her, the soft rise and fall of her chest.

The girl I used to know, wrapped up in a shell that's harder now, but still, that spark is in her. She's still fucking beautiful.

And for the first time in hours, I don't want to break her.

But my mind's miles ahead, already bracing for what's coming. My father.

The fucking empire he's built with blood and violence and everything I've just thrown away. He's not going to let this slide. If you step out of line, you don't just get a warning. You get a fucking bullet. There's no way he'll just let me walk away from this without making an example of me.

I'm his son. He raised me to do his bidding, to follow the fucking rules, to one day take over his empire and I just turned my back on everything he's built. For what? For her?

I pull off the highway, the dim lights of a gas station cutting through the night like a beacon. The place is nearly empty. Just a few trucks parked in the corner, the hum of the lights overhead, and the dull buzz of the pumps.

The car rolls to a stop at the fuel pump, the engine humming to a quiet death as I cut the ignition. I watch her for a beat, her stillness almost too perfect. She doesn't move. I wait, half-expecting her to crack, to reveal the act. Same old game. Pretend to sleep. Keep control. Disappear the second my guard drops.

But there's nothing.

No sneaky move.

No fake breaths.

Just her steady breathing.

When I'm convinced it's not an act, I slip out of the car and press the lock button. One sharp press, and she's sealed inside, a caged bird with clipped wings, trapped in steel and silence, and I'm the one holding the fucking key.

I keep my eyes peeled as I step away from the car, scanning the surroundings. My mind's already ticking, calculating. The shadows, the cameras. I know my father's men will be on me before long, and I'm sure as hell not going to make it easy for them.

The door to the station slides open. I step inside, the stale air heavy. My eyes flicker around, checking the security cameras, counting them in my head. The blind spots, the shadows lurking in the corners, making sure I've got all the angles. Always thinking two steps ahead. I don't trust anyone.

Not now. Not ever.

I move through the aisles like I'm part of the background, just another stranger in a gas station. The flickering lights above, the low hum of the fridge.

I pick up whatever catches my eye. I grab a pack of jerky, something I know she used to munch on when we were younger, before life twisted us into whatever the hell we've become. Some chips. A bottle of water. Nothing special, just things that remind me of her, of what she used to like.

When I reach the back of the store, my eyes scan the rack of cheap sweaters. One catches my eye. A thick, oversized hoodie, just like the one she used to wear when she wanted to hide from the world. Without thinking, I grab it. Maybe it's because she's freezing in that damn thin ass shirt, or maybe it's just the impulse to give her something, anything, to remind her of who she used to be.

I head to the counter with the items in hand, the hoodie tucked under my arm, and the hair dye and snacks in the basket. The clerk's barely paying attention, eyes glued to the TV. Doesn't matter to me. I'm in and out, anyway.

I drop the stuff on the counter. The guy scans it without a word, barely registering I exist. I slide the cash over. He shoves the change back, no eye contact, no effort. I don't say thanks. Just grab the bag, turn on my heel, and head for the door as if none of this ever happened.

I finish filling up the tank and walk back to the car, moving like the world's on pause. I slide into the driver's seat and slam the door.

Emery shifts beside me, and I already know she's awake. I toss the bag her way, careless. Pretending it's nothing. Pretending she's nothing. Even though every part of me knows that's a fucking lie.

"Here," I say, my voice flat, detached.

The bag lands softly in her lap.

"What's this?" she asks, her voice still thick with sleep.

I glance over, just for a second, and my chest tightens.

She's gorgeous, even with the remnants of sleep and dried blood clinging to her. That sleepy look, soft and unguarded, like she's still lost in whatever dream world she's been trapped in.

Memories slam into me... us, seventeen, lying beneath the stars, her hand tangled in mine—both of us too fucking naïve to realize how fast it would all slip through our fingers. We thought we had forever, convinced the world would hand it to us. Believed love could bulldoze through every goddamn thing life threw at us and still come out the other side untouched, beautiful, whole.

I used to wake her like this.

My fingertips in her hair, tucking it behind her ear, as if she were the most delicate thing I'd ever touched. That sleepy look in her eyes... half-awake, half-lost, and still so fucking beautiful it knocked the breath out of me every damn time. The first time I saw her, I didn't believe anything could be that perfect. But she was right there. In my arms. In my world.

I remember walking her home at three in the morning, the cold biting at our skin, but it never mattered. She was the only thing that kept me warm.

I loved her so fucking fiercely, that I'd burn the world down just to make sure she was safe, to keep her from seeing everything I couldn't protect her from. We had no clue how fast it would all fall apart. We thought we could outrun the mess we were born into. Thought we could make it through.

But we were just kids… too naive, too full of bullshit dreams. And now… Here I am, staring at the wreckage of something I'll never get back.

"Some shit to shut you the fuck up," I mutter, eyes locked on the road as I turn the key to start the engine.

I don't wait for a response. Just shift into drive and slam the pedal down. The engine roars to life, and I guide the car back onto the road. The tires bite into the asphalt as I speed off into the night.

The miles blur by. The landscape shifting in the dark. The city's lights fade, leaving only the stretch of road and the quiet hum of the car.

Eventually, I pull off onto a dirt track, the gravel crunching beneath the tires, pine trees closing in on either side. The night feels heavy here… isolated, untouched by the outside world.

This place is mine.

No one knows about it. Not even Salvatore, who's seen me at my worst. The nights when I didn't give a shit who was watching or who I fucked. He's been there, seen me act like I was king of the world in those clubs, losing myself in whatever pussy I could find.

But here, everything's different. Here, I can finally breathe.

I've been running from the empire my father built. The sickening demands, the weight of it all. Every decision, every order, every chain that's been wrapped around me since birth.

I bought this place years ago, under a proxy name, burying it so deep that not a single soul could find it. No one knows it exists, not even my father or his men. It's mine, a quiet refuge where I don't have to bow to anyone's will. A place where I'm not his puppet, doing his bidding like a good little son.

I needed this. I needed it to get the fuck away from his control, the constant pressure to be the monster he made me into. This place is my rebellion, my way out.

I keep my focus on the road as the trees close in around us, the darkness swallowing everything else. The car rolls over the dirt track, the tires crunching beneath, and I finally start to feel that weight lifting. We're almost there. Almost safe.

Then the sharp ping of my phone. It vibrates against my thigh, the sudden noise cutting through the silence of the car.

I don't need to check it. I already know what it is.

The warning system. One of the many alerts I set up around this place to keep me safe. The kind of system that's designed to trigger the second anyone or anything gets too close. Cameras, motion sensors, heat detectors, nothing gets past it.

The trees thin out the closer we get, branches giving way to open space. Then I see it. The house.

Just a shadow at first, then clearer with every second. The car's headlights catch on the dark windows, bouncing off the glass, casting an eerie glow over the yard.

That familiar grip of isolation coils tighter as the driveway comes into view. This place, it's more than just walls and silence. It's a fortress. I don't ease off the gas, just keep driving straight toward the entrance, as if hesitation isn't part of my vocabulary. The place is swallowed in darkness, still and silent. No movement. No lights. Just that kind of quiet that comes from being miles away from anything that even resembles human.

I hit the button on the console, and the garage door groans as it lifts, slow and mechanical. Bright light spills out as the overheads flicker on, illuminating every inch of the polished concrete like a spotlight on the life I never wanted but somehow built anyway.

I ease the car forward, the tires humming as they roll over the smooth surface. The door closes behind, sealing us inside.

The garage blends seamlessly with the rest of the house. It's all clean lines, metal, and glass.

I kill the engine.

For a moment, Emery doesn't move.

She just sits there, eyes sweeping over the space like she's trying to piece together a puzzle she didn't know she was part of.

Then, her voice breaks through the quiet. "Where are we?"

She finally turns to face me, her eyes steady and unflinching.

She's asking what this place is to me. What I am in all of this? And the truth is, I don't even know how to answer.

"This is where we'll be staying," I say, my voice detached, offering nothing more.

I don't wait for her to speak. I shove the door open, stepping out into the cold, and slam it shut behind me. The sound is loud, sharp, and final.

I glance back. She's still in the car, fingers clenched around the bag as if it's the only thing keeping her grounded. For a second, she just sits there, caught between fight and flight.

Then, finally, she steps out.

She scans the garage, eyes trailing over the sleek, lifeless space, as if it's a crime scene. Then her gaze cuts to mine.

"This is your place?" she says, already knowing the answer, just waiting to hear me admit it.

"Does it matter?" I turn away from her, not bothering to look back.

The door to the house swings open with a soft, smooth click, and I step through.

The second I step inside, the shift is immediate. The air itself softens. It's nothing close to the cold, rigid house I grew up in. This place is warm. Lived in. There's a quiet kind of comfort in the way the walls hold the heat, in the way the silence feels full instead of hollow. And for someone raised on violence and expectations, it feels almost unreal.

Soft, golden light spills across the open space, casting a warm glow over rich wood and deep earth tones that wrap the room in quiet comfort. Expensive art lines the walls, but none of it is a power play. It's not here to impress, it's here to make me feel something. Where I can breathe easy. To just be.

It's not at all like the cold marble, hushed tension, and forced smiles that only showed up when there was money on the table. The place I grew up was a cage dressed in luxury.

But this... This feels almost normal. Almost human. And that scares the shit out of me.

I let out a breath. My footsteps echo across the hardwood as I move through the entryway, passing the sweeping staircase that curves up toward the second floor.

Behind me, I hear the thud of Emery's footsteps.

A small smile tugs at the corner of my mouth.

She's not trying to fight me anymore. She's not pushing back, not throwing her smart-ass remarks, or trying to prove she's still in control.

For the first time, something has shifted. It's not a victory born from a fight, nothing loud or triumphant. But still, it's a win. And right now, that's enough.

I move straight to the fireplace. There's no hesitation as I drop to my knees and strike the match. The flame flares to life, catching on the neatly stacked logs, and in seconds, warmth spills into the room, soft and golden. The crackling sound fills the silence, a small comfort in the quiet.

I don't glance her way as I stand. "Shower's upstairs. Third door on the left."

Behind me, I hear the faint rustle of the bag, the creak of the floorboards as she moves. Her footsteps echo up the stairs... slow at first, then quicker.

I just keep staring into the flames, watching them dance like they're trying to deceive me into thinking there's warmth in this fucking cold world. But I feel it in every inch of my skin. The weight of today pressing down on me.

My body, my thoughts, my life, they're all fucking tethered to him. To the man who dragged me into this nightmare when I turned eighteen, branded me, made me a soldier in his empire of blood and fear.

Surely my father has found Rocco by now. He's got eyes every-where. He's been in this game long enough to have every move mapped out before anyone makes it.

He's had me on a fucking tight leash… his hand wrapped around my throat with every move I make. The second I stepped into his world, I stopped being my own man. I stopped having a say. He made sure of that. Made sure I'd always bend to his will, his orders.

So why the fuck hasn't he called? Not a word. Not a message. Just silence

It feels more like a power play. A fucking game he's decided to drag me through for his own twisted amusement. It gnaws at me, eats at my insides, a parasite. The kind of silence that settles over you with the weight of a death sentence.

I'm lost in the weight of my thoughts, when I hear it. Faint. But enough to pull me back.

"Matteo."

The sound of her voice cuts through everything, sharp and clear.

For a split second, everything goes still.

The pressure in my chest tightens. My breath snags, swallowed by a current I can't fight. Hearing my name on her lips, it's fucking familiar, a buried ache tearing its way back to the surface.

I close my eyes, and for a moment, I'm back there.

Back when we were stupid enough to believe we could outrun it all. When she said my name with that kind of reverence, as though it was the only thing that mattered. The way her voice would tremble, soft and so full of love, trusting me with everything she had, with every piece of herself.

I stand there for a moment, trying to force myself to breathe, to push through the thick weight building inside me, and then I hear it. Footsteps. Soft, tentative, like she's not sure if she should approach.

I turn to face her, and everything inside me fucking stops.

Her hair. It's black. The way it used to be.

The way I remember it before everything burned to the ground.

She's standing there, looking at me with those eyes I used to get lost in, and I swear to God—I've stepped back in time. For a second, the years fall away. The girl I loved, so fiercely, so hopelessly, is standing in front of me again.

The rush of memories floods, uninvited, and I can't stop staring at her. I'm that dumb, lovesick kid again. She's that girl burning with fire, pulsing with life, and I'm fucking reminded of the girl who could tear me apart with nothing but a single look.

I swallow hard, fighting the emotions clawing at my throat. The ache in my chest is brutal. She shouldn't affect me this way. I was trained to shut these feelings down. To kill them before anything could grow. Love... Love is weakness. A crack in the armor. My father taught me it was useless—just another way to lose control in a world where control is everything.

But she makes me feel shit I swore I buried. She's the girl I lost... the one I never really let go of. And fuck, I hate how much it hurts to feel that pull again. Familiar. Unforgiving. Like no time passed at all.

Chapter Six

EMERY

There's something in his gaze. Something that throws me off, something that makes my heart stutter in my chest, but I can't place it.

I'm not sure what I'm seeing. It's too... soft, too unexpected. His eyes, those same eyes that once held nothing but coldness and rage, are different now. I don't know if it's just a trick of the light, or if I'm imagining it, but I swear I see something else there.

Something that looks a lot like...tenderness?

I refuse to believe it.

But the way he's looking at me, as if I'm not just a pawn or another name on a list... as if I matter, is messing with my head. It twists what I thought I understood, stirs up things I have no business wanting.

He swallows, before his eyes slip away from mine, as if he's shaking off whatever the fuck that was.

Then, without looking at me, he grunts, "Do you want a drink? Because right now, I fucking need one."

He doesn't wait for an answer. Just turns and crosses the room, each movement is loaded with something he's not saying.

I watch him go, trying to keep my thoughts in check, but it's impossible. Because it's not just the space he's putting between us, it's something deeper.

He heads straight for the bar, fingers ghosting over the bottles with a familiarity that says he's done this more times than he'll ever admit. The soft clink of glass against glass cuts through as he pours the drink. His eyes stay locked on the liquor, not on me, as if it's the only thing worth his attention anymore.

I can't stop watching him. The way his jaw tightens with every move, how the tension coils through his shoulders like it's fused to his spine. He's doing exactly what I've been doing all night. Trying to drown it. Whatever the fuck this is between us. But with every sip, every breath, he's just feeding it. He's giving it room to breathe, to burn, to fucking bloom in the silence.

He fills the glass again and throws it back without a second thought. Then his fingers tighten around the bottle, knuckles white, jaw clenched, as he pours another, chasing the silence he can't seem to find. The war inside him stays unnamed, but it's there, clawing just beneath the surface.

He grabs the bottle of wine and uncorks it in one smooth motion. He pours with steady hands, the wine cascading into the glass, dark and smooth, swirling like blood in water.

Once the glass is full, he lifts it and walks toward me.

He stops in front of me, holds it out without a word, no gesture, no warmth. Just his eyes on mine. That calculating stare that strips me bare and leaves the air thick with something I can't name.

"Drink," he commands, his voice rough.

He doesn't move. Just stands there, watching, eyes fixed on mine, unblinking, as if missing a moment would cost him something.

I raise the glass to my lips, and his stare hits me hard, a weight that's impossible to ignore.

The wine slides over my tongue, smooth but burning hotter than it should under the weight of his stare. Every nerve lights up. It's raw, exposed. His eyes stripping me down without ever touching me.

He watches me swallow, gaze fixed on my lips as if he's cataloging every breath.

My lips part as I take another sip, and I catch it, that flicker in his eyes.

It's dark and dangerous. His gaze drops, locked on my mouth like he's already imagining his there, tasting the wine off my tongue.

It's a silent kind of hunger, and it shouldn't make my heart race,but it does. A twisted rush of want and warning, pulsing through me, a secret I don't know how to bury.

I feel the heat of him, a storm rolling in fast, pressing against me without a single touch. I should turn away. I want to. Before this slips past the point of no return.

But I don't.

There's a war waging inside me. A brutal pull between shoving him away and dragging him closer. My chest tightens with every breath he takes. And somehow, in this unbearable silence, I can feel it. His heartbeat syncing with mine. A rhythm we shouldn't share. But we do.

I see the tension coiled in his shoulders, the twitch of his fists like he's fighting every instinct screaming at him to close the space between us. He's holding himself back, as though restraint is the only thing keeping him from unraveling. And just when I think the silence might snap from the weight of it, he reaches out, takes my glass, and sets it down beside his.

Then he leans in. His face hovers inches from mine, breath warm and uneven, daring me to be the one to move first.

And for a second, I swear he's going to kiss me. His breath ghosts across my skin. His lips are right there, so close it hurts, hovering just out of reach. The world narrows to this moment, to the space between us, to the single fucking breath where everything stops and is about to change.

His eyes flutter shut, breathing me in, the nearness too much, too close, and still not fucking enough. His jaw clenches, and I see it, the way he's losing himself in this, in me, in the unbearable pull that's been simmering beneath the surface for too long.

It's not just want. It's surrender. Silent and shaking.

But then, just as quickly as he let himself feel it, he looks away.

His face hardens.

He takes a step back, and the space between us isn't just physical anymore, it's fucking miles.

When he speaks, his voice is cold enough to cut. But buried underneath is something darker. Something that sounds a hell of a lot like regret.

"Your room's upstairs," he says, his voice rough. He doesn't look at me when he says it. "At the end of the hall."

I watch him leave, his footsteps heavy as he moves up the steps, never once glancing my way. He's distancing himself, pretending I'm not here. But the tension doesn't fade, it lingers, thick in the air, a storm waiting to break.

I'm left here, alone with the thudding in my chest, the echo of his absence loud in the silence. I want to call after him, ask him what the hell's going on in that fucked-up head of his, but I don't.

Because I know it won't matter. He's already closed off, the door already slammed between us the second he turned away.

Matteo's footsteps fade into the distance and still I wait, my pulse roaring in my ears, the tension crawling beneath my skin, itching to burst out. I don't move... just hold my breath, praying for the moment when the silence tells me he's gone. That he's finally left me alone.

Seconds pass. Minutes, maybe. But when I finally convince myself he's not coming back anytime soon, I snap into motion.

My heart pounds in my chest as I race through the house, feet thudding against the polished floor, my head spinning with every turn, my mind screaming at me to find some way, any way, to get the hell out of here before he decides to drag me back into whatever fucking game he's playing.

I get to the front door, my hand trembling as I reach for the keypad beside it. My fingers fumble for the code, his code. I don't know it, but desperation drives my hands, pressing random digits in a frantic attempt to unlock it.

Beep. Nothing.

Fuck. I try again.

The cold metal of the keypad under my fingertips feels like a fucking mockery now.

Beep.

Another failure.

Frustration tears through me, burning fast and wild. The walls feel tighter with every breath, my hands trembling, clawing for a way out. The code's nothing but a dead end. I'm locked in a goddamn box, no exit, no mercy.

I turn away from the door, my heart racing as I look for anything else. Anything that will give me even the slightest chance to break free. My eyes dart around the hallway, searching for an escape route. They land on the windows.

I race toward them, hoping, praying, there might be a way through. I reach the first one, pressing my hands against the glass, my palms cold against the smooth surface. I try to push it open, but there's no handle. And it won't even fucking budge.

I step back, a wave of panic rising in my chest as I move to the next window. The same thing, this floor-to-ceiling glass shit with no way out, no escape.

I'm trapped. The walls, the windows, everything is designed to keep me in. Every inch of this house is a fucking trap.

I take a step back, my throat tightening as the weight of it hits me. There's no way out. No fucking way.

He's got some fucked-up security system, probably tracking every goddamn movement, every breath I take. I can almost feel him laughing, some sick amusement dancing in his eyes as he watches me scramble, watches me fall apart.

I'm the rat in his maze, stuck with no way out, no fucking hope. And he's sitting there, getting off on some twisted fucking satisfaction as I fail, as I break down piece by piece. I'm just a fucking game to him.

No one's coming for me.

Not now.

Not ever.

The silence makes it real. The kind that doesn't echo... it just settles. Like dust and the truth. I should've known better than to believe I was someone worth saving. But hope's a cruel fucking thing.

Chapter Seven

Matteo

I sit back in the leather chair, the soft glow of the security monitors flickering before me, each screen feeding me her every move.

Emery. Her movements are frantic, desperate.

She's yanking at doors, slamming her palms against windows, her body tense with the realization that there's no fucking way out. But there's something in the way she moves, something that keeps pulling my eyes back to the screen. The way her frustration boils over, the heat in her gaze, the fire that burns beneath it.

I can't help but admire her, despite the irritation creeping up my spine. There's something mesmerizing about the way she moves. Even in her panic, there's a grace to it, a raw energy.

For a moment, I almost gave in. The temptation to taste her again was unbearable. I could almost feel her breath on my lips, the warmth of her body against mine. The way my cock was screaming for me to take her, to claim her. But I shoved the desire down, locking it away.

I can't afford to lose control. Not now. She's a fucking distraction.

A beautiful, fiery distraction that keeps pulling me in, testing every fucking wall I've built around myself. But that's all she is right now. A distraction. A threat to my focus. I can't afford to get lost in her again. Not when my father's a breath away from hunting me down, when I need every ounce of my wits to stay one step ahead of him.

I shouldn't have gotten that close to her. Shouldn't have leaned in, let my mouth hover near hers. But I did. And now I'm paying for it.

My cock's still hard. Still fucking pulsing. A painful, steady throb that won't let me forget what I walked away from. And while I sit here, trying to get my shit together, my dick has other plans. It aches with need, screaming for attention, for release, for her.

She settles onto the couch in front of the fire, legs curled up, eyes fixed on the flames like they're going to give her all the answers I couldn't. Her face softens, her body stills, and for a second, the world around her slows down too.

I stay where I am, unmoving, jaw clenched, chest tight. Watching. Waiting.

Trying to fucking breathe through it.

The flames flicker, casting a warm glow across her skin. She looks like a fucking painting, something soft and unreal.

I stay frozen, watching her, my heart fucking pounding. Each throb of my cock is a taunt, a fuck-you from my body for trying to do the right thing.

When she finally goes still, settles like she's given up for the night, I move.

I head straight into the bathroom, flick the light on, and lock the door behind me. I strip my clothes off, each piece feeling toxic, soaked in too much of her, and I can't fucking stand it on my skin. I turn on the shower, wait just long enough for the water to steam, then step in. The second the spray hits, scalding hot, hissing against my skin, I don't flinch. I need it. I need something to sting, something sharp enough to cut through the chaos clawing inside my chest.

But it doesn't help.

Not even close.

My cock's still pulsing, acting on its own. It's hers now, not mine. Tuned to the curve of her mouth, the sound of her breath when I get too close, the way her eyes burned through me, full of intention, like she knew exactly what she was doing.

I brace a hand on the wall, my forehead pressed to the tile, and wrap my tattooed hand around my cock. The first stroke is rough. Too rough...but I don't fucking care. I need to feel something. Need to burn the tension out of me, to claw back some kind of control.

But there's no escaping Emery.

Every thought slams into me with every movement of my hand... her lips, her neck, the way she looked at me, as if I'm something more than just a fucked-up mess. As if I could be wanted.

I jerk harder, faster, water pounding down my back, heat coiling low in my gut, a fuse burning fast. There's no rhythm. No control. Just raw, reckless need—filthy and fucking furious.

Every part of me is aching, coiled tight, chasing that high like I'm starving for it.

"Fuck..." I grit out, teeth clenched, hips snapping forward into my fist, desperate for more—more friction, more feeling, more of anything that'll drown out the rest.

And then it hits.

I come with a guttural noise torn straight from my chest. It's loud and broken. A punishment ripped from somewhere deep. There's nothing soft about it—nothing slow. It hits hard, a goddamn explosion, hot and violent, splattering across the wall, the water washing it away before I've even caught my breath.

I stand there after, braced against the tile, chest heaving, water pounding down over me like it's trying to wash away everything I just felt.

But it can't.

Because Emery's still there. Burned into every fucking inch of me. And no amount of release is enough to make her disappear.

Steam curls around me, but I don't move. My head stays bowed, hand still gripping the wall—the only thing keeping me upright. My heart's still pounding, even after unloading every ounce of want that's been building inside me since the moment she walked back into my life.

But it didn't help.

The ache's still there, low in my gut, my body knowing exactly what my mind's trying to bury. Because no matter how hard I came, I still fucking want her. Not just her body. Not just the sound of her gasp when I get too close. I want all of her. The parts she hides. The pieces she doesn't give to anyone. The parts I used to know better than my own skin... and all the new ones that scare the shit out of me, because they don't belong to me anymore.

I shut the water off, and the silence in the bathroom hits hard, a punch to the chest. I grab the towel off the hook, dragging it over my face, down my tattooed chest. It's rough and fast, as if I can scrub the need off my skin.

I throw on a clean pair of jeans and yank a shirt over my head, still damp, still fucked. My hand hesitates on the doorknob to my bedroom, jaw tight. For a second, I consider locking it. Staying in here. Hiding from her. From myself.

Instead, I open the door to my bedroom, and head downstairs. Every step is heavier than it should be. Like gravity's doubled just to fuck with me. When I hit the last step, I see her. She's still, curled up on the couch, bathed in firelight, A soft blanket draped over her legs. Her eyes watching the flames.

She exhales slowly, and when she speaks, it's soft. Almost like she's talking to the flames instead of me.

"Did he really sell me out?"

She doesn't look at me. Doesn't need to. Because that question, it's not just about betrayal. It's about every moment that led her here. Every scar her father carved into her life when he handed her over like she was some bargaining chip.

"Yeah," I say. "He did."

She doesn't flinch. Doesn't cry. Doesn't even fucking move. Just stares into the flames, trying to convince herself that saying it out loud will dull the truth. But her jaw's tight, her grip on the blanket tighter—every muscle straining to hold herself in one piece. Because if she lets go, she won't survive the break.

"When?" she asks, voice barely above a whisper.

"Two days ago."

The silence hums, sharp enough to cut. She keeps her eyes on the fire, holding steady, because looking away might be the thing that finally breaks her.

"How?" A pause. "How did he sell me out?"

I swallow hard, the answer sticking in my throat. "He put your name on the table," I say, voice low and raw. The kind of rough that scrapes your throat on the way out.

I move toward her, slow, each step like I'm walking through a goddamn minefield. I sink into the chair across from her, elbows on my knees, and look straight at her.

"One of my father's men caught wind of it," I continue. "He heard your father was reaching out. Trying to make a deal to buy his way out of a death sentence. Word was, he had something rare. Something personal. Something valuable." I pause, jaw clenched tight. "That something was you."

She doesn't speak. Doesn't even blink.

She just sits there like marble, frozen, flawless, breaking from the inside out.

"He was cornered," I finally say, even though it makes me sick to say it. "The walls were closing in. He knew my father wanted blood," I go on, slower now, more careful. "And he knew he couldn't outrun it. So he gave them you. One of my father's men made the call. He told them where to find you. Your alias. The address. Place of work. Packaged it neatly, wrapped in a bow, and handed it to the highest bidder. The truth is your father put your life on the market to save his own. He knew my father would jump at the chance to see if you had the information he was after."

"But he should know your father won't stop," she mutters, voice tight, like she's chewing on rage just to keep from falling apart. "Not until he gets what he wants. That's not how your father works, he doesn't stop until the end. How fucking stupid for mine to think he could sell me out and buy himself time. It won't matter. Your father will keep hunting him, Matteo. He'll burn everything down just to find him."

She turns to look at me, and the firelight flickers in her eyes, catching every fractured piece of her. Her stare holds mine.

"My father never wanted a daughter," she says, her voice flat, emotion stripped bare. "I've been nothing but leverage to him since the day I was born. A pawn in his sick, twisted game."

She doesn't blink. Doesn't waver. The words fall out, not as a confession, but a fact—cold, carved in stone. Something she's carried forever, just waiting for someone to say it out loud.

And I feel it.

The way it hollows her out. The emptiness that one truth has carved into her. The weight of it's been pulling her under for years, and I'm just now seeing how much space it's taken up inside her.

She turns back to the fire, her gaze flickering with the orange glow.

"That's why I left that world," she says, her voice softer now, edges fraying with the weight of her words. "When your father pulled you deeper into his empire, I knew it was only a matter of time. He'd take whatever softness was left in you and crush it. And when he did..." She exhales, slow and shaky, like the weight of the past is pressing down on her. "You'd be gone. Lost to me. And I wouldn't be able to reach you anymore."

My gut twists, like a raw wound reopening. Because she's not wrong. She saw the rot creeping in long before I ever tasted it. She saw the darkness that would swallow me whole, and she tried to save me from it.

"I watched it happen, Matteo. I saw it in your eyes before I left. You were already slipping away."

For a moment, I can't breathe because her words are the truth. They cut deep. Because I became exactly what she feared. Hard, cold, unreachable. I let myself drown in that world, and she was right. I became a stranger to myself.

"I knew he'd make you into something I couldn't save," she says, her words cutting through the air. "That one day you'd look at me and not see the girl you used to love, but just another weakness to be discarded."

It hurts like hell, hearing her say that. Because in her eyes, I was never the villain. I was the boy who could've made it out. The boy who chose not to. And that's what fucking kills me.

Not the blood on my hands. Not the bodies I stepped over to survive. What haunts me is the way she looked at me back then, with that stupid hope in her eyes, convinced I was still worth saving. And the worst part... the way she's looking at me now, full of everything I never became. Everything I could've been. Should've been.

And maybe she's right. But now it's too fucking late to become the boy she believed in.

CHAPTER EIGHT

EMERY

I've been sitting in the same spot for what feels like hours. And all I can hear, on repeat, is Matteo's voice, spelling out the truth like it was nothing. How my father put my name out there, knowing exactly what that meant. Knowing Alessandro DeLuca, Matteo's father, the goddamn king of blood-soaked vendettas, would slit my throat without blinking. No hesitation. No mercy. Just a name on a list. Just leverage. Just me.

I've always known my father was disappointed in me. Hell, it wasn't a secret.

The disappointment started the second I was born, when the doctor said, "It's a girl," and his dreams of a loyal little monster to carry his name died right there in the delivery room.

He wanted a son.

Someone he could mold into a weapon.

Someone cruel and cold, cut from the same brutal cloth.

He followed Alessandro De Luca's orders without question. Matteo's father wasn't just powerful, he was the power. The kind of man whose name carried weight in every room, whose silence alone could break weaker men. He didn't need threats. He didn't need violence. He taught my father everything he knew. How to lead without mercy, how to control without raising his voice.

Because when Alessandro De Luca spoke, the world listened, and when he didn't, it trembled.

My father was his loyal dog. His blade in the dark. The one who did the dirty work, spilled the blood, kept his hands steady while other men broke, begged, bled. He never questioned. He never flinched.

Until he did.

Until greed, fear, and desperation snapped whatever loyalty he had left. And just like that, he went from asset to liability. From trusted to hunted.

And when he ran, he didn't run alone. He dragged me down with him, tied me to his sins, an anchor I never asked for.

That day... my father looked me in the eyes and told me to run. Told me to fear for my life, because the monsters were coming. Told me to vanish so deep, so far, that even the ghosts wouldn't find me.

And I did.

I ran until my legs gave out, until the fear became a constant hum in my bones. I didn't go to Matteo. I couldn't. Because even back then, I knew I'd already lost him. He was too far gone, swallowed by that world, bleeding himself dry just to earn a nod from the man who never once saw him as a son.

Matteo was busy proving he could be the monster Alessandro De Luca needed.

Not the boy who used to trace promises on my skin.

Not the boy who said he'd never let anything touch me.

Not the one who kissed me like I was his only truth in a world built on lies.

Matteo buried that softness, choked it out of himself one order at a time. Every scar, every shattered look in his eyes, was just another step closer to becoming the man his father could finally be proud of. A soldier. A weapon. A loyal fucking shadow. And maybe that's the part that hurts me the most. Is that I was never enough to make him stay the boy he once was. Not when he could be his father's perfect creation instead.

I'm so fucking pissed I can't see straight.

Not at Matteo. At him. My father.

If what Matteo said is true and I don't doubt it, not with the way he's got me locked in this life like I'm collateral. My father has sold me out. Traded my life to save his own. And now I'm the one left carrying the weight of his betrayal. The one paying the price for a deal I never agreed to.

He whispered my name into the dark, fully fucking aware it would reach Alessandro De Luca's ears like a signal flare. He knew what he was doing. Knew they'd come for me. They'd get me no matter the cost. He didn't just throw me to the wolves. He gift-wrapped me. Laid me at their feet with a bow on my back and a knife buried deep in my spine. And when they came for me, I bet he didn't even flinch. Didn't hesitate. Just watched the flames catch, lit the match himself, and called it strategy.

All while I burned.

And now...

I wonder if he thinks I'm dead. If he sleeps better pretending my bloods already soaked into someone else's floor. If he closes his eyes and imagines a body bag zipped shut with my name on it.

Maybe that's easier for him. Cleaner. No guilt if the problems already buried. But I'm not in the ground yet. I'm still here thanks to Matteo, still breathing for how long, I do not know.

A sound snaps through the silence. My body jolts before my mind catches up, instincts yanking me out of the chair and into the shadows—pure muscle memory. Every breath feels too loud, a betrayal in the quiet.

Matteo left hours ago. Said something about supplies. Something to eat. He didn't look back when he said it. He just disappeared into the night.

Now the silence, it just feels... different. Tighter. Tense in a way that scrapes against my skin. It feels off.

I press myself against the cold wall, heart pounding against my ribs like it's trying to claw its way out. For a second, I wonder if this is it. If De Luca's men have finally found me. Or if Matteo never planned on coming back.

Or worse... if he led them right to me.

My pulse spikes as the sound comes again. It's closer this time. Then I hear footsteps. Measured. Unhurried. Like whoever it is knows I have nowhere to go.

I scan the room in a panic, eyes darting for something, anything.

A weapon. A defense. A fucking chance.

My gaze lands on the fireplace poker leaning beside the cold hearth. I move fast, quiet, grabbing it with trembling fingers, the weight of it both reassuring and completely useless against men who know how to kill without blinking.

The footsteps grow louder...heavier.

Closer.

Each step punches through the silence like a warning, a promise, death dressed in leather shoes and patience.

I press myself tighter into the corner, the poker clutched in white-knuckled hands, breath locked in my throat.

And I wait. For a face. For a reason to swing.

The footsteps pause, just on the other side of the wall.

My breath stutters.

My grip tightens on the fireplace poker.

My heart hammers, pounding out a warning… run, fight, fucking do something.

Then a shadow moves first, stretching across the floor. I don't hesitate. I swing. Hard, fast, all instinct and fear. The poker whistles through the air, aimed for a skull, a throat, for something.

But the bastard moves fast, jerking back just in time. And in the split second it takes me to recover, a hand lashes out and grabs my wrist, tight enough to make my fingers go numb.

"What the fuck, Emery?"

Matteo.

His voice is low and furious, jaw tight, eyes burning into mine like I just betrayed him. He yanks the poker from my grip and lets it crash to the floor.

He stares at me, as if I've lost my goddamn mind. His grip tightens around my wrist, just enough to remind me who's in control. His eyes, cold and dark, bore into mine, searching for the truth, trying to rip it out piece by piece.

"I thought we were past this shit," he snarls, voice like gravel and gasoline. "You think I dragged you out here just to put a bullet in your fucking skull?" He steps in closer, heat radiating off him, fury bleeding through every word. "If I wanted you dead, Emery, you'd be in the fucking ground already. What the fuck is wrong with you?"

"Next time maybe don't sneak around like a fucking predator, Matteo."

He stares at me. Not with anger. Not entirely. There's something else simmering behind his eyes, something darker, hungrier. I swear for a second, he leans in.

It coils low in my stomach, that look—uncertain, dangerous, torn between slamming me against the wall or fucking me against it.

Then he blinks. And just like that, the spell breaks.

He lets go of me.

The loss of contact hits hard, cold and sudden, as if he took something with him the moment his fingers left my wrist.

He turns and walks further into the room. The bag slung over his shoulder lands on the counter with a solid thud. Food. Supplies.

He doesn't look at me. Just reaches into the bag, pulls out a takeout container, and sets it down on the edge of the counter, closer to me than to him.

"Penne with extra garlic," he mutters, voice low and rough, as if saying it out loud costs him something. As if he's trying to make it sound casual.

But it's not. He remembers. Not just the dish, but exactly how I like it.

And that shouldn't matter. But fuck, it does.

He turns back to unpacking the rest, like he didn't just toss a memory between us and walk away from the fallout.

I move to the counter, close enough to feel the tension radiating off him, but neither of us says a word. It hangs there as if we breathe wrong, the whole thing will crack wide open.

Matteo opens a drawer and pulls out a fork. He sets it on top of the container without looking at me, without saying a word. He's not trying to take care of me... but he still is.

His head stays down, pretending to focus on unpacking the rest of the bag, pretending the food suddenly matters. Doing everything he can to avoid looking at me.

So, I look at him. Really look at him. For the first time.

He's changed.

Sharper around the edges, more shadows in his eyes, more silence in his movements. But he's still him. Still Matteo.

His hair's a little longer than I remember. Messy like he ran a hand through it too many times. His jaw is tight, the kind of tension that's lived there for years now.

But it's the ink that catches my attention. Just above the collar of his shirt, peeking out along the side of his neck. Black lines and shadowed edges, curling up his skin.

I don't recognize this one. It's new. Bold. A piece of him that wasn't there before. A piece of the life I wasn't around to witness. A piece of something private he never meant anyone to see.

And God, he's beautiful in the way only something broken can be. In the quiet way he exists in this room, full of shadows and restraint. He's different now, harder, sharper, but somehow still familiar.

"You done eye-fucking me, Em, or should I take my shirt off and save you the trouble?" His voice is smooth, sharp, lethal in that low drawl that coils heat straight through my gut. "I mean, if you wanna drop to your knees, sweetheart, just ask."

"If I wanted to drop to my knees, Matteo," I say, voice laced with wicked intent, "I'd already have your cock down my throat, and you'd be the one begging me to let you come."

His breath stutters, just once. Almost imperceptible. But I see it.

The way his jaw locks. The way his fingers curl into fists at his sides. Like he's holding himself back by a thread, and I just lit a match.

His eyes burn into mine, all darkness and restraint barely hanging on. "You think I'd beg?" he growls, voice rough and lethal.

"I don't think," I purr, voice sweet and slow, "I know." I step a little closer, letting the words hang in the air like a challenge. "From memory, you used to beg me not to stop when I sucked your cock," I tease, my eyes locked on his. "So, tell me, what's changed, Matteo? Or are you just too proud to admit you want me to do it again?"

His eyes flare, pupils darkening as the words hit him like a punch. He breathes out, rough, barely a growl, and for a split second, I see it, the moment where he almost loses it.

"If you think I'm about to beg, you're fucking delusional," he snarls. "If we fuck, it's nothing more than me getting off. Nothing more than me using you like I always have."

"You can keep pretending it's nothing more than a fuck," I say, my voice cold. "But we both know that's a lie."

I watch his eyes, the flicker of anger, the hesitation behind the mask he's trying to wear.

I smirk, grabbing the takeaway container with all the fake calm I can muster as if I didn't just set the air on fire between us.

Then I turn, walking away slowly.

Every step is a reminder.

Every sway is a tease. And I make damn sure he sees exactly what he's not getting.

"Thanks for the penne," I say, tossing a look back at him over my shoulder.

His eyes burn into me, and I feel the heat of his gaze as it follows me across the room. I can practically feel the frustration radiating off him, and I fucking love it.

Chapter Nine

Matteo

S he walks away as if her words didn't just light me the fuck on fire. My breath is ragged, chest heaving, every inhale a fight, every exhale burned out from the hit.

I don't think. I move. Because there's no pretending anymore. No holding it back. Not when I've already come undone for her a hundred fucking times since she's been back in my orbit.

She's halfway down the hall when I catch up. My hand wraps around her arm as I yank her back toward me.

Her breath catches, but she doesn't fight it. Doesn't flinch. Like she knew I'd come.

She opens her mouth, but I don't give her the chance to speak.

My mouth crashes to hers. It's brutal, hungry, all teeth, heat and fire.

I kiss her to punish her for walking away. To mark her from the inside out. Because fuck pretending. Fuck restraint. It's the kind of kiss that says, you started this... now fucking feel it.

I press my hips forward, grinding against her, letting her feel exactly what she's done to me.

My hands thread into her hair, deep, possessive. I feel the silky strands tighten between my knuckles as I wrap my fist in it and yank her head back. Not hard. Just enough to remind her who the fuck she's dealing with.

Her spine arches slightly, her neck is bare, and fuck, if that doesn't undo something primal in me.

"I warned you," I growl, my mouth dragging against her jaw, my grip firm in her hair. "You don't throw words like that at me and expect me to play nice." Her pulse pounds at her throat. "You want to push me, baby? Fine. I'll take it out on you with my cock."

She gasps, soft, involuntary and it shoots straight to my cock like a goddamn lightning strike.

No hesitation. No filter. Just pure, unfiltered need punching through me, hard and fast. One fucking sound from her, and I'm already on the edge.

I drag my mouth down her neck, teeth sinking in just hard enough to leave a mark, just hard enough to claim her.

Her hand fists in my shirt, a desperate grip for control that's already slipping through her fingers. And she knows it. She's burning in the same fire she set off in me.

My free hand slides down her back, gripping her ass, hauling her hips hard against mine. She can feel what she's done to me. The thick length of my cock straining against my jeans, demanding more. Demanding her.

"Say it," I whisper, biting at her earlobe. "Say you fucking want it."

Her breath stutters.

I feel it, hear it, right against her throat. That shaky exhale she tries to hide but can't. It shudders out of her, body straining under the pressure, smart-ass mouth finally catching up to the fire she's been playing with.

And fuck, I love it.

Love that I'm in control. The way her pride is slipping through her fingers. The way her body presses into mine like it's not even a choice anymore, but more like it's instinct.

I bring my mouth to hers, close enough to feel her breath, to taste the heat between us... but I don't kiss her. Not yet. I want her trembling for it. Begging. I want her to feel the ache of almost, the burn of everything she can't have until I say so.

I just stay there, brushing her lips with mine, letting the tension stretch tight between us. She leans in, just barely, chasing it. Needing more. Chasing the kiss. The fucking kiss I won't give her.

Her brows pinch, confusion flashing in her eyes for a second, but I see the truth written all over her face.

The need. The want, the desperation.

"Uh-uh," I murmur, tightening my grip in her hair, pulling her head back slightly so she's forced to look at me. "You don't get to start fires and expect me to hand over the match."

She lets out a soft, frustrated sound. Part breath, part moan... but it only makes me smirk.

"You want my mouth?" I growl, eyes locked on hers. "Then fucking say it." I grind against her, making sure she feels exactly what I can give her. "Say you want me to fuck you."

Each word is a dare.

A promise.

A threat wrapped in desire.

She squirms, just a little, and it's fucking beautiful. Her body's screaming yes while her pride still tries to claw its way through.

"Come on, baby," I growl against her jaw. "You're already soaked through. You're already shaking for it. Don't play innocent now."

I drag my lips over her throat, not kissing, just hovering, letting her feel how close I could get if I wanted to. Letting her burn in it.

"Do you want my cock, or are you just going to keep pretending this is a game you can win?"

She swallows hard, eyes locked on mine, her pride flickering.

And then, she speaks, it's barely a breath, a whisper. "Yes."

I don't move. I don't kiss her. Don't even ease the tension.

I tip her head back, baring that perfect line of her throat, and it's mine. Every inch. And fuck, she knows it.

My voice drops, a growl against her skin. "Tell me what you're saying yes to."

She exhales, it's shaky and soft. She's strung tight, wound like a bow ready to snap. My hand clamps down on her hip, fingers digging in, claiming, marking. I want her right there, on the edge. Mine. Desperate. Seconds away from begging me to ruin her.

"Say it, Emery," I murmur darkly against her skin. "Don't make me drag it out of you."

She closes her eyes, jaw tightening like she's trying to hold on to something, but it slips...finally, and when she opens them again, she's done pretending.

"I want you to fuck me, Matteo" she breathes. "Hard."

And right there, she gives in. It's in her eyes, in the way her breath hitches and her body leans into mine like she needs it.

I smirk.

It's slow, dangerous, and full of promise.

The kind of smirk that says I've fucking won.

Because I have.

And we both know it.

Those words were the shift of power. The second her pride slipped through her lips and gave way to need. Now I've got her right where I want her.

"You make it too easy," I murmur. "Didn't take much to break you, did it?"

Her lips part, trembling, ready to lie. Ready to pretend she hasn't already given in.

But I tighten my grip in her hair, just enough to make her gasp. Just enough to remind her exactly how deep she's already buried in this. In me. And there's no crawling out now.

"You play a good game, baby," I growl, tilting her chin higher. "But two can play just as dirty."

Her lips part, her chest heaves, and fuck if I don't want to devour her right here, right now. Pin her to the wall and take her hard until her thoughts are nothing but shattered fragments, until she's moaning my name like a prayer and forgetting every reason she ever had to resist. Fuck her senseless, until the only thing she knows is me. My hands. My mouth. My cock. And the ruin I leave behind.

It takes every starving inch of me to let go of her hair. It's ripping claws from something I'm not ready to release.

Her eyes snap up, wide and wild, heat still smoldering beneath the confusion. She looks wrecked. Wanting.

On the edge of something feral and fucked, and I swear if she begged right now, I'd ruin her without a second thought. But this is about power.

I let her go. Fingers still twitching with the ghost of her. Then I turn, force my feet to move toward the kitchen, jaw clenched, cock hard enough to ache.

Every fucking inch of me is screaming to turn around. Grab her. Haul her upstairs and rip every stitch of clothing off her like it's a fucking offense to my hunger. I want to fuck the ache out of me.

Instead, I plant my hands on the kitchen counter, muscles coiled so tight I'm shaking with it. My whole body's humming, aching like it's been denied oxygen.

I shift, trying to breathe through the tension, but the pressure's fucking savage.

The only goddamn relief I'm getting tonight is with my own hand wrapped around my cock. And fuck... even that won't touch what I really want.

Her. Bent. Begging and ruined.

Chapter Ten

EMERY

Fuck him. Seriously, F.U.C.K Matteo for that smug, manipulative shit he pulled last night.

He made me beg. Beg for his touch, his cock, like I'm some desperate little thing starving for it. And then he just walked the fuck away, left me aching, wet, wrecked.

No more of that shit. If this asshole wants to play…Then I'll fucking play.

I stand in front of the mirror and rip off the oversized shirt I slept in, let it drop to the floor. My nipples are already tight from the chill, from remembering how he made me feel last night.

Yep, this will fucking do.

I run my eyes over my body, my tits on full display, the black lace panties that barely cover anything. He wants to be in control than he has to remember who the hell he's dealing with.

I walk out of the spare room. Tits bare, chin lifted, every inch of me daring him to look. Daring him to crave me the same way I wanted him last night.

The hardwood bites at my soles, but I don't stop. Don't flinch. Not when the fire in my chest is hotter than anything underfoot.

I move through the house like smoke, slow, sinuous, sexy, untouchable.

The moment I step into the main area, I see him. Back to me, body wound tight, eyes fixed on the floor-to-ceiling windows. Waiting for something to break, for the outside world to cave in. Ghosts. His father. Or worse... his father's men. The kind who don't knock. Just kick the door in, dragging bullets and blood behind them.

I watch him closely, silent. His jaw's locked, every line in his face pulled tight, a storm just under the surface.

This isn't distraction. It's preparation. He's bracing for the hit—for the door to blow open, for that unseen danger to finally show up and put a bullet between our eyes.

And now I feel stupid, like he bruised more than just my ego last night, and I'm the idiot still aching from it, already plotting how to make him feel it too. I came out here with a plan. To rattle him. To steal back the power he yanked from me last night.

But now, looking at his back, I see it, the weight he wears, fused to him, impossible to shake. This isn't loud fear. It's the kind that sinks in deep. Quiet. Heavy. Coiled tight, a fuse just waiting for the right spark to rip everything apart.

He's not just tense. He's scared. Of what's out there and how close it's getting.

Maybe he pushed me away last night because that's the only way he knows how to protect me, by pretending he doesn't care before it all goes to shit. Or maybe he just didn't want me. Not like the way I wanted him.

What the fuck am I doing? This isn't me.

I'm not the girl who plays power games with her tits out, flashing skin like a lure and hoping he'll bite.

No. When I fight, I use what counts. My wit, my strength, the fire I had to build bone-deep just to survive men like him. I don't beg easy. And I sure as fuck don't break.

I should turn around. Walk away before this spirals any further. Let this whole fucked-up plan crash and burn right here, with my pride barely clinging to what's left of it.

I start to turn, to walk away before I unravel right here in front of him.

But then... he turns. And just like that, every part of me that was ready to run forgets how.

And the second his eyes land on me... fuck. Everything just stops.

Not the room. Not the air. But me. Like my pulse forgets how to beat, my lungs forget how to breathe. My whole body short-circuits under the weight of that stare. It's burning, brutal, and made of every unspoken thing we've both been trying to outrun.

His gaze crashes into mine, trying to gut me open, searching for the weak spot I haven't shown anyone in years. Then it drops... slow. Too fucking slow. Scraping down every inch of my skin, dragging over the places he used to touch, tasting the memory of it.

There's something in the way he looks at me that makes me feel already on my knees. He's replaying every second of how I wanted him last night, committing it to memory, not for nostalgia, but for precision. So he can break me better this time. Ruin me right.

And I hate that I'm still standing here, burning alive under his eyes, wondering if his cock's as hard as the look he's giving me right now. Wondering if that stare means he still wants to fuck me... Or just finish what he started.

Either way, I know I'd let him. And that might be the most fucked-up part of all.

It hits before I'm ready. That stolen breath. That full-body betrayal. Goosebumps flare across my skin, heat and hunger tangled up in one sharp rush. My nipples tighten, tuned to his eyes, aching, needing, desperate for the touch that isn't there yet.

And then I see it hit him, in the way it catches in his throat. The hard swallow. The twitch in his jaw. That flicker in his eyes, something feral breaking loose.

His hands flex at his sides, and fuck, it's all there. He doesn't know if he wants to reach for me as if I'm holy, something to worship... or something to ruin.

Then slowly, his gaze drops down to the lace. To that thin strip of black clinging between my thighs, barely there, delicate as breath and twice as dangerous.

His stare lingers, heavy, with weight behind it. Pressure and promise rolled into one. He hasn't moved. Hasn't spoken. Hasn't even blinked. But my body's already responding, obeying some unspoken command. It remembers, every time he touched me. And worse, every time he didn't, but should've.

His lips part, just barely, but it's enough.

Enough to make my stomach twist into knots. Enough to make my thighs clench—they already know what's coming. Then his tongue flicks out, slow and deliberate, dragging across his bottom lip as if he's tasting me from across the room.

My breath stutters, and I fucking hate how much power that stupid little move has over me. But it's him. It's always been him.

Then he shifts, subtle, but I catch it. The slight roll of his hips. The way he adjusts his stance, like his cock's too hard, too heavy to ignore, straining against the denim, begging, starving for release. I wonder if it's twitching. If it's already leaking.

Is he imagining pushing me up against the wall, tearing the lace from my thighs and burying himself deep, hard, ruthless?

And now all I can think about is what he'd do if I closed the distance. If I dropped to my knees and gave him exactly what that ache is screaming for. Because I'm aching for it too. I feel my pulse everywhere. Between my legs, under my skin, in my throat.

My nipples are tight, aching, and the heat between my thighs is unbearable. I'm fucking soaked. Shamefully so. Like my body's already decided for me.

Then he moves toward me, all heat and hunger in motion, every second without me written in the tension of his body.

The space between us disappears in seconds and when he reaches me, it's not soft. His hand fists in my hair, dragging my head back just enough to force my eyes to his...and fuck, the look in them. He's not just looking at me. He's consuming me. Like he's already fucking me in his head, deciding exactly how he's going to make me fall apart.

"You've been playing with fire, baby," he mutters, voice thick with want. "Now you're going to burn."

His mouth crashes onto mine, no warning, no hesitation.

All teeth and tongue and raw hunger.

I gasp into it, already drowning, already behind.

This isn't a kiss. It's a fucking claim. He doesn't just want me, he needs me. I'm the fix after starvation. The thing his mouth was made for. And now, there's no hiding it. I'm his to ruin, to wreck, to consume by his hands, his tongue, his cock and he's done pretending otherwise.

A moan rips out of me when his arm snakes around my waist, dragging me tight against him.

He's all heat and muscle and sin, a solid fucking wall I never stood a chance against. And then I feel him, hard and thick, grinding into me through denim like his cock's trying to carve its shape into my body.

Holy fuck.

He's huge. And he's not being subtle about a damn thing.

I swear my knees would give out if he wasn't holding me up, pinning me to the heat of his body, with that brutal, caged need radiating off him like he's seconds from snapping.

"You feel that?" he says against my throat, voice all low and dark, shredded from restraint. "That's what you fucking do to me."

He thrusts again, harder this time, grinding the thick length of him right against the pulse between my legs. And fuck…my head tips back, eyes fluttering closed as heat coils in my spine, sharp and aching. Then his lips brush my throat, soft and wicked.

"You walk around as if I won't bend you over the nearest surface and fuck you so hard you'll forget your own fucking name."

My fingers claw at his shoulders, desperate to hold on, trying to anchor myself—but there's nothing steady left.

No ground. No breath. Just Matteo. Just the chaos he's pulling me into. The way he's dragging me out of my own body and turning me into something that belongs to him.

"Tell me," he growls, mouth hot at my ear. "Tell me how fucking soaked this sweet little pussy is just from thinking about my cock buried deep in it."

A sound tears from me.

It's needy, a whimper pulled straight from my gut. Because fuck yes, that's what I want and I don't care that he knows that. I don't care that he can feel the heat rolling off me or the way I'm clenching around nothing, like my body's already begging to be filled.

I'm not hiding this anymore. Not the way I tremble. Not the way I throb for him. Not the way I want him to split me open and never let go.

His hand slides between us, fingers dragging slow over the curve of my hip, carving it into memory.

"I'll have you begging for it," he breathes, his voice rasping against my skin, rough as sandpaper, scraping into places I didn't know could ache.

He rolls his hips again, slow, but punishing. Deep. Deliberate. Trying to fuck the breath from my lungs without even being inside me yet.

My gasp stalls in my throat. My back bows, body synced to his without a choice.

"And when I finally fuck you Em…" he growls, lips brushing the shell of my ear, each word sharp enough to leave marks, "you'll be thanking me for every goddamn second I made you wait."

His fingers dig into my hip, possessive, like he's branding me, marking what's his. His body is all heat and tension pressed against mine, and my lungs barely work with the weight of him so close.

Then he leans in, his mouth brushing my ear, voice rough and commanding.

"Take out my cock."

My pulse stutters. Every part of me clenches at the way he says it—low, filthy, a dare wrapped in heat and control. Daring me to defy him.

"You want it, don't you?" he murmurs, grinding against me. The hard line of him leaving no question. "You know you've been thinking about it. Fucking aching for it. So take it out."

I swallow hard, my fingers already moving, shaky and eager, fumbling with his belt like I might fall apart if I don't get to him fast enough.

He watches me with fire in his eyes, his breath hot against my cheek.

"That's it. Don't fucking stop."

And fuck, I don't. I can't. Because this... him, has me undone before I've even wrapped my hand around him.

His hand snaps around my wrist the second I free him, rough and deliberate, making me gasp. His cock is heavy in my hand, hot, hard, and fuck, he knows exactly what he's doing. He knows the effect he has on me.

He leans in again, his voice nothing but filth and dominance, low and dark right against my ear.

"Get on your knees," he growls. "Suck my cock."

The command does something to me.

There's no hesitation.

No room for thought, just raw, fucked-up need.

"I've let you tease me long enough," he says, his tone sharper now, dragging his thumb across my lower lip. "So get the fuck down there and do what we both know you've been dying to do."

My knees hit the floor before I even realize I've moved. He lowers his gaze, watching me with that wicked smirk of his. Like he owns the world, and maybe me in this moment, too.

"Open that pretty little mouth of yours," he mutters, his hand threading through my hair, his grip tightening. "And don't fucking stop until I say so."

My lips part, breath shaky with want as I lean in, wrapping my fingers around the thick girth of his cock. He's burning hot, and hard as fuck. His veins throbbing under my palm, already slick at the tip with pre-cum.

I drag my tongue around it. Slow, teasing. Lapping up every drop like I've been starving for it. Then I take him deeper, letting my mouth slide over his cock, wet and hungry, until my lips stretch wide around him.

The second I do, he growls. It's low and filthy. His hand twisting in my hair like he's already losing control.

And shit, that sound he makes... That sound fucking wrecks me.

"Fuck, that's it, baby," he breathes. "Your pretty little mouth looks so fucking good wrapped around my cock." His hips jerk forward just slightly. Controlled but needy, and the sound he makes, rough and ruined is enough to send heat spiraling between my thighs.

"Take it all," he commands. "Take every fucking inch I give you. I want to feel your throat around me. I want to feel you choke and show me how much you want this." His voice is filthy, feral, and dripping with need.

Every word has me sinking lower under his spell. Has me hollowing my cheeks as I take him deeper, addicted to the way he shudders.

"Fuck, that mouth was made for this," he groans, head tipping back. "It was made to be used."

And right now, I want nothing more than to let him use it.

His grip tightens in my hair, not enough to hurt, but enough to hold me there.

Enough to remind me who's in control.

His cock twitches on my tongue, and when I glance up at him through my lashes, the look he gives me is pure fucking sin.

"Keep your eyes on me," he says, his voice rough with restraint. "Don't fucking look away."

I do as I'm told, my lips wrapped around him. My mouth stretched full as he begins to move. Slow at first. Shallow thrusts that let me feel the weight of him, the drag of his cock across my tongue.

"Fuck, that's it," he breathes, jaw clenched, sweat already starting to gather at his temples. "God, your mouth... it's like you want to be fucking ruined."

He thrusts a little deeper, groaning when he feels the back of my throat, his free hand bracing against the table behind him. "Yeah, take it, baby. Let me fuck that mouth."

And he does.

He rocks into me, each stroke longer, deeper, more deliberate. My throat tightens, tears prick at the corners of my eyes, and I moan around him. It's needy, wrecked, addicted. The sound makes him hiss through his teeth, hips jerking forward with a rough snap.

"Fuck, that noise," he growls. "That little whimper says it all. You need my cock down your throat."

I don't pull away.

I can't.

Not when he sounds like that. Not when his cock is heavy and slick with spit, fucking into my mouth—owning it.

"Look at you," he groans. "On your knees for me, mouth so full of cock you can't even think straight. Bet you're dripping down your thighs right now, aren't you?"

He slows his thrusts, just slightly, pushing in deep and holding it there, watching my lips stretched tight around him, my throat fluttering as I fight not to gag.

"Fucking perfect," he murmurs. "You were made for this. And I'm not stopping until I come in that gorgeous mouth."

And with the way he's fucking me. Deep, claiming, relentless. I know he means it. His thrusts get rougher, more desperate, more possessive, like he's barely holding on. He holds me steady, guiding me, using me, his cock fucking into my mouth with precision.

"Fuck," he grits out, his voice fraying at the edges, breath ragged. "You're gonna make me come... fuck... you want that, don't you? You want me to lose it down your fucking throat."

His hips snap forward, and I feel him pulse, hard and hot, right at the back of my throat.

"Fuuuccck," he groans, loud, raw, wrecked.

His head tips back, the muscles in his thighs going tight as he unloads. His cock twitching as he spills into my mouth. Hot, thick, and so much. He doesn't stop until he's spent and panting. His hand still tight, gripping my hair like I'm the only thing keeping him grounded.

"Jesus fucking Christ," he breathes, looking down at me with blown pupils and a ruined expression. "That mouth... fuck."

I swallow every drop of him, lips still wrapped around him until he finally eases back. His fingers slowly unwind from my hair, but his hand lingers, brushing along my cheek, gentle now, almost reverent, like he's not ready to let go. From the dark, wild look in his eyes, I know he won't.

He eases back just enough, slowly pulling his cock from my mouth, watching the way my lips cling to him until the very last second. His chest rises and falls with every breath, sweat at his temples, cock still slick and hard despite what he just gave me.

He strokes himself slow and unbothered, gaze trailing over every inch of me, weighing his options, deciding whether to worship me or wreck me.

"Get that pretty pussy up on the table," he says, voice rough and full of heat. "Now."

I don't move right away. I'm stunned, shaking, still tasting him on my tongue.

He steps closer, hand still wrapped around his cock, the head flushed and dripping. "Don't make me say it again."

I scramble to obey, my body already moving before my brain catches up. I slide onto the table behind him and lean back on my hands, chest rising fast, heart pounding. Loud. Relentless. It knows exactly what's coming.

And fuck, I want every second of it.

His gaze is dark, hungry, devouring. He steps between my legs, pushes my knees wider, lips wet with anticipation, uncertain what he's going to do to me first, only that he will.

"I haven't decided yet," he mutters, voice dripping with filth and control. "I might feast on this sweet little cunt 'til you're crying. Or I might just slide my cock into you and fuck you stupid."

He bends forward, face inches from where I'm already soaked, already aching.

"Either way, baby," he breathes, "you're not leaving this table without being ruined."

Chapter Eleven

Matteo

She scrambles onto the table like a good fucking girl, her body moving without question, thighs parting just enough to tease me with a glimpse of everything I'm about to corrupt. The cold surface makes her flinch, but she doesn't say a word. She just leans back on her hands, chest heaving, lips parted, eyes wide with that mix of want and surrender that drives me wild.

My cock's hard, throbbing with every breath she takes. I tell myself not to touch it.

Not yet.

Not until I've earned it. But one look at her, and my hand's already wrapping around my cock, giving it a stroke, needing the feel of it to keep from losing control.

She deserves to be devoured first. Ruined properly. With my mouth, hands, tongue. Every fucking part of me wants to taste her before I even think about sinking inside her. Because when I finally do... I'm not fucking stopping until she forgets how to beg for anything but me.

I step between her legs, dragging my hand up her thigh. Slow enough to make her squirm. She's soaked already, dripping, and I haven't even touched her properly yet.

"You're fucking trembling," I mutter, voice low and rough, thick with promise. "And I haven't even put my mouth on you yet."

I sink to my knees without flinching. No shame in it. No hesitation. She's the only one who's ever made me fall this hard. The only one who's ever owned me without even trying.

This isn't surrender. It's control. Because even on my knees, I own every fucking second of this. And she knows it.

Her breath hitches and her hips shift forward like her body already knows what's coming.

I lean in, breath hot against the mess between her thighs, close enough to taste the want dripping off her.

"Let me make this crystal fucking clear," I grit out. "I'm not here to tease. I'm not here to play. I'm gonna make you come on my tongue. Not once. Not twice. I'm gonna eat this pretty little pussy until you're soaking this fucking table. Until your legs give out and all you can do is whimper my name like it's the only fucking word you can remember." I drag my tongue slow over my bottom lip, eyes locked on hers. "Then maybe...maybe I'll think about giving you my cock."

She lets out a sound, half whimper, half moan and that's all I fucking need. My grip tightens around her thighs as I drag her to the edge of the table. She belongs there. Because she fucking does. Right here. Spread wide. Mine to feast on. And right now... I'm going to fucking prove it.

My face hovers just above that tiny scrap of lace. It's soaked, clinging, pointless really because it's not hiding a damn thing.

I breathe her in. Fuck. That scent slams into me, sweet, hot, soaked in need. I close my eyes, just for a second, and breathe her in. Filling my lungs with what already belongs to me. Because she does. Every desperate inch.

She shifts. Just a twitch in her thighs. But I see it. Feel it. She's panting already, trying like hell to stay still.

I look up at her, my lips curl into a wicked smirk. "You smell like heaven," I say.

I hook a finger through the waistband of her panties, eyes locked on hers. No hesitation. No mercy. I tear that soaked little scrap in half. It never stood a chance.

Her bare, glistening pussy hits me, pure adrenaline straight to my cock. I drag my stare down, drinking her in, jaw clenched with restraint I have no intention of keeping.

"And I'm about to fucking destroy it," I bite out. "You're so fucking beautiful," I snarl, voice rough as sandpaper, my hands tightening around her thighs as I shove them further apart. "Now keep those legs wide open, be a good little slut, and let me taste every filthy inch you've been keeping from me."

And then I'm on her. Mouth pressed to her pussy, starved, desperate. My tongue drags through her heat, slow at first, filthy and possessive. I'm not just eating her. I'm owning her. One fucking mouthful at a time.

She moans, loud and unfiltered. Her fingers claw for the edge of the table, back arching, hips twitching like she can't help herself.

Good. Let her feel what she does to me. But I'm not stopping. Hell, I've barely even fucking started. She wanted the storm…I'm about to tear her world apart.

I drag my tongue over her again… long, slow, filthy, from the slick heat of her entrance all the way to the top, pausing at her clit just long enough to make her whimper.

Then I pull away. "Stay still," I command, voice low and razor-sharp. "You move before I say, and I'll fucking stop."

My grip tightens, pinning her open, mouth hovering just above the place she's already throbbing for me.

"Be good, baby," I murmur, lips brushing her skin, "or you won't get to come on my face until I say so."

She freezes, breath caught, thighs twitching, her whole body strung tight beneath my grip.

So fucking perfect.

I smirk. And then I get to work.

I flatten my tongue and drag it through her slowly. Long deliberate strokes. I don't rush. I don't need to. Every flick of my tongue is a statement. A claim.

She whimpers, her hips trying to rise, but my hands lock tighter around her thighs, keeping her pinned wide open for me. She's at my mercy... exactly where she belongs.

I lick her again and again. Slower this time, just to feel her shudder. Just to hear the way her breath turns into broken little moans. Her thighs quake when I circle her clit, lazy, teasing, just enough pressure to make her gasp and not nearly enough to let her come.

Her pussy's soaked, trembling under my mouth, and all I can think is how fucking good she tastes. How she's dripping for me like her body knows I'm the only one who gets to have it.

I keep circling her clit. Slow, lazy strokes, tongue working her like she's the only thing I'll ever want in my mouth again.

She gasps. Hips twitch. But she doesn't move.

Good girl, she's fucking learning.

I groan against her, the sound rumbling deep in my chest and vibrating straight through her soaked pussy.

She cries out. It's sharp, broken, and fucking perfect.

It's a sound that wrecks me. A sound I'll chase until she's trembling and begging for more.

"Already so fucking sweet," I mutter against her pussy, licking her again. This time slower, more filthier.

I slip my tongue down, teasing her entrance before dragging it back up, just to flick her clit and hear that fucking sound that tears from her throat.

"You keep dripping like this," I growl, licking harder, licking deeper, "I'll be down here all fucking night."

And I mean every goddamn word. Because this... This isn't about getting her off. It's not even about making her come until her legs stop working. It's about possessing her. Tongue first. Cock second.

Because she doesn't get to just feel this. She gets to remember it. Every time she breathes. Every time she closes her eyes. Every time she thinks of pleasure... It's me.

She's gasping, her legs trembling in my grip, body teetering on the edge, seconds from snapping.

Every time my tongue flicks over that swollen little clit, she lets out a broken sound. It's breathy, like she's being torn apart from the inside. And fuck, I feel her fighting it. Trying to behave. Trying to be good.

I pull back just enough to blow a slow, warm breath over her soaked pussy, watching it twitch, every nerve in her body mine to command.

Then I drag my tongue up the center, sucking her clit with just the right pressure to make her writhe. Her taste floods my mouth, the only thing I was ever meant to consume. She was made to come on my tongue.

I'm not just feasting on her. I'm fucking memorizing her. Claiming every fucking inch of her pussy with my mouth.

She lets out a whimper. It's soft, shattered, soaked in need.

"Say it," I growl, lips brushing her inner thigh, voice sharp and low like a promise she better keep. "Tell me who this pussy belongs to."

Her head tips back, fingers clawing into the table like she's holding on for dear life.

"You, Matteo," she moans, voice breaking. "It's fucking yours."

That's all I need. I snarl, raw and feral, before I slam my mouth back on her, no teasing, no mercy, just pure fucking hunger.

My tongue's unrelenting, worshiping her. She's the altar, and I'm the sinner who finally found salvation. I lick her with purpose, with need.

This is where I belong. Just filthy devotion, over and over, until she falls apart for me.

I wrap my lips around her clit and suck hard. My tongue rolls over her, working her in a rhythm that's punishing and perfect. Her hips jerk, thighs clamping around my head, desperate, shaking, caught between ecstasy and overload. She doesn't know how to survive this, and I don't let her try. I grip her tighter, holding her exactly where I want her. Right here. Right on the edge.

"Don't come," I growl against her. "You come before I say, and I'll fucking edge you until you're crying for it. All fucking night."

She lets out a cry, muffled by her teeth sinking into her bottom lip, her body practically screaming for release. But I don't let up.

I fuck her with my tongue, slow at first. Then hard and fast. Switching pace just to watch her twitch. Just to hear her pant my name like a prayer that only I answer.

She's soaked. Shaking. Desperate. She's trembling so hard, it's a miracle she hasn't come already, right here on my fucking tongue.

Her legs are locked tight around my shoulders, thighs shaking, her whole body riding the edge like it's about to break. Her hips twitch, trying to grind against me, instinctual, and if I wasn't holding her down, she'd be fucking my face right now.

Every time I touch her clit just right, she gasps a sharp, broken, breathless little sound that only makes me hungrier. She's right there. I can feel it.

In the way her pussy flutters against my tongue. I glance up through my lashes and fuck me, she's gone. Her eyes are glassy. Her chest is heaving. Her lips part around silent moans. She's ruined. Unraveled. Feral for it. And it's the most beautiful fucking thing I've ever seen.

I slide a finger into her. It's slick, hot, gripping me. Then I add another, stretching her open, fucking her slow and deep while my tongue keeps working her clit.

Her whole body twitches, too sensitive to take it, too desperate to want anything else. Then I curl my fingers just right, pressing into that spot that makes her legs jump and her hips jerk off the table.

I do it again.

Deeper. Harder. Faster.

Her walls clench around me, pulsing—her pussy trying to pull me in, keep me there, make me part of her fucking soul.

She moans, the sound torn from her lips as she slips out of reality.

"Come for me," I growl, voice a razor scraping across her skin. "Now."

She doesn't just come, she fucking detonates.

Her body locks up first, spine arching off the table like she's being torn in two. A cry rips out of her throat. Then she falls apart on my tongue.

Her pussy clamps around my fingers so tight like it's trying to hold onto me, trying to keep me there while the orgasm tears through her, a goddamn storm. Her legs tremble, then jerk. Then shake. I don't care. Her whole body convulses, again and again, every muscle short-circuiting under the weight of it. This isn't just release, it's collapse. Total surrender.

And I don't fucking stop. Not while she's twitching. Not while she's sobbing my name like it's the only thing she remembers.

Her hand flies to my hair, pulling hard enough to make me growl. She's loud, wild, fucking feral with it.

"Stay with me, baby," I mutter against her. "Don't run from it."

I hold her through it, licking her slowly, my tongue dragging over her clit just to feel her twitch. To hear her whimper through the overstimulation. Her hips try to twist away as if it's too much, but I hold her tight, keeping her right there.

She gasps, legs trembling uncontrollably, her whole body flushed, wrecked and drenched.

When Emery finally collapses against the table, boneless and trembling, she's panting like I've fucked her into another world.

I rise slow, unhurried, every muscle vibrating with satisfaction. I wipe my mouth with the back of my hand, my eyes never leaving her, already plotting how I'll break her all over again.

She's still all over me. I can taste her. Feel her. Breathe her.

And my cock... It's a fucking riot, straining, throbbing. Painful in a way that dares me to lose control. I haven't even touched myself, and I'm already riding the edge like I could snap with a single stroke.

I look down at her. She's so perfect. Hair wild. Lips swollen. Chest rising and falling, still chasing breath. Her thighs are spread wide for me, glistening and open—her body unwilling to close, unwilling to forget. Even now, after everything, she's mine. Still offering. Still needing. Still fucking mine.

And fuck if I'm not about to take it.

"You have no idea what you've just fucking done to me," I snarl, grabbing her jaw hard enough she feels it, tilting her face up until her eyes lock with mine. "And don't get comfortable, because I'm not even close to being done with you."

Her eyes flutter open. There glazed. Like she's floating somewhere between bliss and breakdown.

And that look... Fuck. That look tells me everything. She'd let me take her again and again. Until her legs give out. Until her voice breaks. Until the only thing she knows is the way I had her falling to pieces.

And now that I've started... I'm not stopping until she's ruined for anyone else. Until every part of her aches with the memory of what I did to her. Until her body knows the difference between being fucked and being owned.

Chapter Twelve

EMERY

I can barely breathe. My body's still twitching and wrecked from the last orgasm. From his mouth, his voice, the way he devoured me like I was the first taste of something he'd been starving for.

Now he's standing over me. Looking down. Cock hard, jaw tight, eyes burning, seconds from snapping.

"Get off the table," he says. It's a command, not a request. That growl laced into every word that makes my pussy clench all over again.

I get onto my unsteady legs, my thighs slick and shaking, yet still somehow not close to being done.

The way he's looking at me, he's about to fuck the rest of his control straight into me. And I know... this is only the beginning.

The second my feet hit the floor, he's there. Hands on my waist, spinning me with a force that steals the breath from my lungs. He drives me forward until I slam into the wall, cold and sharp against my skin, but there's no time to flinch.

He's at my back, all heat and muscle, pinning me between him and the cold, unforgiving wall.

One hand fists in my hair, yanking just enough to tilt my head, bare my throat, make me his. The other slides between my legs. His fingers slipping through my slick pussy like he already fucking knows what he'll find.

He groans, low and filthy, the sound vibrating against my skin.

I'm a mess. Dripping and desperate, my pussy already begging to be split open by his cock. I can't fucking breathe until he's inside me.

"I should make you beg for this," he murmurs, voice a low scrape of danger against the shell of my ear, a threat dressed up as a promise. His lips brush my neck, slow and deliberate, leaving heat in their wake, branding me without teeth.

"I should fuck you slow," he breathes. "Make you feel every inch. Make you earn it for what you just did to me." His grip in my hair tightens. His cock grinds against my ass, thick and hard. "And maybe…" He leans in, teeth biting my skin now. "Maybe I fucking will."

I arch without thinking.

My palms flatten against the wall, bracing myself, heart slamming in my chest like it's trying to break free.

"But I've waited long enough, Em."

One hand grabs my jaw, firm, demanding, forcing me to lookup, right into those dark, furious eyes. Eyes that say he's about to fuck the life out of me.

"You ready for it?" he snarls. "You want me to fuck you now?"

And God, the way he says it… low, rough, like a fucking dare wrapped in a warning… I already know the answer.

I feel it in my chest, in my spine, in the heat pooling low and fast. Every inch of me is already his. Begging to be claimed.

I can't speak. I just nod, lip caught between my teeth, chest rising in shallow, broken breaths.

That's all it takes.

He grabs his thick, aching cock and drags the swollen head along the curve of my ass, smearing precum like his marking me.

His arm locks around my waist, lifting me without effort. He positions me where he wants me, spread, trembling, desperate to be filled.

"Fucking soaked," he mutters, cock grinding between my legs. "Dripping down your thighs like this pussy's been waiting for me to fill it."

He spreads me open, no hesitation, just lines me up, and presses the thick head of his cock right against my entrance.

"Take a breath, sweetheart," he growls into my ear. "Because I'm not giving you time to adjust."

And then he dives in.

One brutal thrust. Balls-deep. No mercy.

My forehead rests against the wall. My nails scrape down the surface as I stretch around him, stuffed full, pussy clenching hard like I don't know whether to take more or fall apart.

I scream, like I've never screamed before.

His chest presses to my back, breath hot against my neck. "You feel that?" he says. "That's me splitting you open. Just like you fucking asked for."

And then he starts to move.

"Fuck," I choke out.

His mouth is at my ear, breath hot, voice ragged and low. "You feel that?" he barks, cock buried to the hilt. "That stretch? That ache?" He thrusts harder, and I gasp. "That's how deep I get. Only me. No one else. No one fucking else puts you back together and tears you apart in the same breath."

Another thrust.

He fucks me with the desperation of a man starved too long, wild, relentless, a fury born of need and memory. My body's no longer mine. It's his. And he's not letting go. Not now. Not ever.

Matteo's cock drives deep, stretching me past the point of pain, into that place where pleasure turns into something primal. Something that burns. I can't tell if I'm breathing, falling, or flying.

His grip on my waist is bruising, pinning me to the wall.

"Fuck, you take me so good," he snarls against my neck, voice ragged, hips slamming into me with brutal force.

The wet, filthy sound of skin on skin echoes through the room, loud, raw, shameless.

"You're so fucking tight," he grits, biting down on my shoulder. "You were made for this cock. You were built to fucking take me."

And the way he drives in again, deeper this time, harder, it's like he's trying to put me through the wall.

I cry out as my front slams into the wall with every brutal thrust. He fucks into me hard, ruthless, each drive a claim. A mark. A demand that I never forget this, that I feel him every time I breathe. Every time I fucking move.

There's no thought left. No air. Just the stretch, the relentless force of him filling me so deep. It's perfect.

"Matteo…" I gasp.

He growls behind me, low and feral, grabbing my thigh and hauling it higher. And then, fuck, he angles deeper.

I shatter with a moan, head dropping back onto his shoulder as he fucks me harder and harder with every thrust. It's rough and controlled. Every thrust landing right on that spot that makes my whole body seize up. Every snap of his hips sends stars exploding behind my eyes. And still, he's not letting up.

Not when I'm gasping. Not when I'm clenching around him. Not when I'm whispering his name like a prayer I'll never recover from.

Because Matteo doesn't just fuck. He claims. And he's claiming every inch of me right now.

"I told you I'd ruin you," he says, voice all grit and fire. "And look at you. Fucking begging for more."

My body's already shaking again. Pressure coiling fast and brutal in my core along with the scream trapped in my throat.

I'm close. Too close and he knows it.

He sinks his teeth into my shoulder, biting down hard enough to make me cry out. His hips slam into me, relentless, filthy... each brutal drag of his cock pushing me right to the fucking edge.

"You gonna come again, Em?" he growls, reaching in between my legs, fingers finding my clit.

He rubs rough and perfect, with just enough pressure to make my knees buckle.

"You gonna come all over my cock like a good little slut?"

I try to speak. Try to say something but all that comes out is a whimper. Because I am ready to come like a good little slut and nothing can stop it.

My body breaks as I shatter around him, hard, crying out as the orgasm tears through me like it's trying to split me open from the inside.

I clamp down on his cock, pulsing tight, desperate, my legs trembling, too weak to hold me steady. My vision whites out. The world vanishes, only him remains. Matteo, buried deep, relentless, fucking me through every crashing wave, carving himself into me with every thrust, branding his name into my fucking bones.

And still he keeps fucking into me.

His growls turn filthy as he chases his own release. His thrusts turn rougher, faster, more desperate. His breath is ragged, his skin slick with sweat, muscles tight as a bowstring.

"Fuck... Emery," he chokes, voice wrecked.

Then he slams into me one final time, buried to the hilt, so fucking deep and he breaks.

He comes with a guttural sound torn straight from his chest, years of restraint breaking in one brutal moment. His whole body shudders, cock twitching deep as he empties himself, hands locked around my hips in a bruising grip, terrified I'll disappear mid-fuck.

We stay like that, completely wrecked. I can still feel him inside me, every twitch, every pulse. My body doesn't know how to let him go. I'm shaking, breath shattered, skin slick with sweat and sex. Branded. Ruined in the best fucking way. And I'd take it all over again just to feel him lose control for me.

The only sound is our breathing, rough and uneven, hearts pounding out of rhythm, like neither of us has quite come back to earth yet.

The silence stretches. His body still pressed to mine, the room dim and still, the air warm with everything we just gave each other.

And yet, there it is. That feeling I swore I'd buried.

It hits soft at first, like breath against skin.

Then deeper.

Heavier.

That ache I've carried for him. The love I tried so hard to forget. The kind that hurts more than it heals.

I thought I walked away from it. Told myself it was the only way to protect what was left of me. Told myself he was too far gone, too walled off, too broken for me to reach anymore. His father had won. Molded him into exactly what he wanted. This cold person, he could control. Lost and untouchable to me anymore.

But here I am, his body still inside mine, his breath ghosting against my neck and that feeling is back. That quiet, steady pulse of something I never stopped feeling. God, I loved him. I still fucking do. Even when I swore I'd moved on.

He moves, just barely. One hand drags slowly up my side, over my ribs, over the curve of my waist, until his palm rests flat over my stomach. Not possessive. Not rough. But just there.

His mouth finds my shoulder. Not with hunger. Not with heat. With something else. Something softer.

He presses his lips there, slow and warm as if he's holding a memory between us, afraid it'll slip away if he breathes too hard. His breath ghosts across my skin, and then his lips find me again. It's softer this time. A tiny kiss lands on my shoulder, full of hesitation, as if he's not ready to let go.

And for a second, just one quiet second, it feels like love. The kind that never needed words. The kind that never really left. Just a kiss that lands deeper than any thrust ever could.

And I feel it.

Not dominance.

Not control.

But recognition.

He remembers. What we were. What we lost. And maybe, for one fleeting second, what we still are.

And standing there, chest aching, heart wide open in the arms of the only man I ever truly loved. I realize the scariest part isn't that I still feel it. It's that he feels it too, even if he'll never say it out loud.

CHAPTER THIRTEEN

MATTEO

Eight Years Ago

I'm seventeen.

One more fucking week till eighteen.

One more week till I'm supposed to be a man when I don't even know how to fucking breathe yet.

It already feels as if life's got its boot jammed against my throat, pressing down harder every time I try to lift my head. I'm bleeding out slowly... one dream at a time.

The weight of it sinks into my bones, tattoos itself into every fucked-up inch of me. Heavy in my chest. Heavy in my blood. Like every scar I've seen, every bruise I've earned, is being sewn into my skin with wire instead of thread.

When I'm lying next to Emery, the world fucking stops. The weight doesn't vanish, it's still pressing on me, but it freezes. The universe hands me one goddamn second to feel. To breathe. To exist. To remember I'm not just the machine my father made me into. I'm more than the weapon. I'm still human. At least with her.

For this second, I'm not his heir, his weapon, or his fucking puppet. I'm just a seventeen-year-old kid. A kid who still wants things he's not supposed to want.

She smells of wildflowers and midnight... the kind of scent that makes you believe in something again. The only thing worth living for. Peace in the middle of a war zone. She's a lullaby in a world that never stops screaming, pulling me into something softer. Something real. Something I never thought I'd fucking get.

And for just this moment, I let myself pretend. I pretend I'm not drowning in the mess my father made of me. I pretend I'm not bound to a life I can never escape.

I pretend that maybe I can just be me for a fucking second. A boy who loves a girl who makes the noise in his head a little quieter. A girl who makes every bit of the pain, the darkness, the brokenness, a little less sharp.

But I know it won't last.

Because a love this fierce... this pure... it isn't meant for someone like me.

Emery's head is resting on my chest, her hair moving with the wind. The stars above us stretch on forever, like they were thrown across the sky just for us.

For once, the world isn't fucking screaming. It's not bleeding or burning. There's no blood on my hands, no ghosts clawing at my conscience. Just the sound of crickets, the soft rustle of leaves, and the rhythm of her breath against my skin.

I close my eyes for a second, letting myself believe it's real, that I'm not trapped in the chaos I've always known.

It's so peaceful.

Peaceful in a way that makes me wish I could stay here forever.

I draw her closer, wrapping my arm around her, the last thread holding me together. I need her more than air. More than I'll ever admit, even to myself. Her warmth sinks into my skin, quiet and steady, and for a moment, I wonder if she's the only reason I'm still standing.

Emery's so goddamn beautiful it's suffocating—just looking at her feels like drowning. Reaching for something you already know you'll lose, but you reach anyway. Desperate. Hoping she won't slip through your fingers. It's in the way her body fits against mine, seamless, like she was built for this. For me.

The steady rise and fall of her breath calms something wild in me, like maybe the storm in my chest can finally go quiet. And when her eyes flutter shut, it's not the big moments that break me. It's the quiet ones. The little things. They wreck me completely.

The way her lashes kiss her cheeks. The tiny mole tucked under her jawline that only I ever see. The faint curve of her lips when she smiles makes everything else disappear. The blood on my hands. The ghosts in my chest. When she looks at me, she doesn't see the monster, I swear she sees something worth saving.

And fuck, I'd set the whole goddamn world on fire just to keep her looking at me like that. Just to keep that tiny, reckless piece of her believing there's still something good left inside me.

I want to shield her from everything. From the shadows that follow me. Because she has no idea. No clue about the blood I'm gonna spill. No fucking clue about the choices that already have my name carved into them.

And still, she lays here, unfazed, as though I'm not the hurricane ripping through everything good and pure in her world. It's in moments this quiet, when no one's watching, when it's just her, me, and the stretch of endless sky, that I let myself believe in the lie. That maybe... I am the boy she sees when she smiles.

And fuck, I want to be.

More than I fucking want anything

"Matteo," she whispers, her voice soft. "Do you think we'll ever get out of here?"

I don't answer. I can't. What the fuck am I supposed to say to that?

Instead, I drag my fingers through her hair, as if I can smooth the weight out of her voice. Maybe I can fucking fix something for once. Her hair slips through my fingers, all silk and softness. Too good. Too pure. Too fucking untouched and innocent for hands that only know how to destroy.

But I know what she's really asking. It's not about this place, or the four walls closing in around us. It's about everything. The chains we were born into. The blood we didn't get to choose. The way our fathers carved their sins into our skin before we even knew what the fuck we were even becoming.

She's not asking if we'll ever leave this town. She's asking if we'll ever outrun this life that has made us who we are. If we'll ever tear free from the noose already tightening around our throats. If we'll ever be more than the fucked-up futures someone else stitched into our bones.

Fuck, I want to promise her. I want to swear to her that we'll burn it all down and build something new with what's left of us. But the truth sits heavy on my tongue. I don't know if there's a way out. Not for kids like us. Not when the darkness is already part of our goddamn bloodstream.

"We'll get out," I lie, the words scraping my throat raw. But I say them anyway—because it's what she fucking needs. My voice is rough, but I force it steady, willing it to sound real. "We'll leave all this behind," I tell her. "I'll take you anywhere. Anywhere you want."

By anywhere I mean that isn't carved out in blood and betrayal. Because if anyone deserves a life beyond this goddamn empire built on blood, it's her. She's too good for this, too innocent, too beautiful to see exactly what it is, and if there's even a sliver of a chance that life still has room for me... then I'll bleed for it. I'll burn for it. I'll tear my own fucking soul apart for a life with her.

She tilts her face up to mine, her eyes locking onto me like she's searching for something buried in the ruins. And for a second, I forget how to breathe. She's always been able to do that to me. Always been able to look past the sharpened edges, the broken, rusted-out parts I don't even have the guts to name.

"Promise?" she whispers, and it's not just a word. It's a fucking lifeline, frayed, trembling, clinging to something that has no place in our world. It's hope. And goddammit, I want to reach out and grab it. Wrap both hands around it and give it to her, even if I know it'll tear me apart in the end.

I nod. "I promise."

It's a fucking lie, and I'm sure she knows it. But it's all I have left to give her, a promise built on broken bones and burned-out dreams. I won't let her see it. Not tonight. Not when she's curled against me, breathing like I'm still something worth believing in. I'll carry the lie for her. I'll fucking drown in it if it means she gets to keep dreaming a little longer. Even if it fucking guts me.

Her father's been my father's right-hand for as long as I can remember. Bound by something uglier than loyalty. Blood spilled in dark corners, secrets buried in shallow graves, deals carved into flesh before I even drew my first breath.

Two monsters dressed in matching suits. Suits steeped in violence, stitched together with power and blood. Built not to serve. To destroy.

And us... We were born into a world already choking on smoke and violence. Where love is a weakness and trust is a loaded gun.

My father never lied to me. He didn't need to. He fed me the truth in fucking fists and fire, pain a rite of passage, blood a twisted inheritance. He dragged me through it, teaching with bruises, branding lessons into my skin until there was nothing left to question.

Through alleys slick with blood, past the bodies that no one ever bothered to bury. Over floors where the screams were swallowed whole by the silence.

He didn't shield me. He prepared me. But not for the future. He prepared me for a goddamn war.

While other kids were out there kicking soccer balls, scraping their knees on the pavement, I was learning how to scrub blood off my hands before it had time to dry. I was taught how to shut down the part of me that flinched, the part that still cared.

Because in his world, weakness was a death sentence. And I couldn't afford to be weak.

He said it was the only way I'd survive this world. That softness, was suicide. Mercy... just another bullet waiting to find its way into my chest. He taught me that kindness wasn't noble, it was fucking fatal.

Every time I hesitated, someone else wouldn't. And in our world, hesitation is a goddamn death sentence.

I've pulled the trigger. Watched grown men cry, beg, even piss themselves. Stared down the barrel of a gun with eyes so fucking empty that I couldn't even remember what it was like to be a kid who hadn't yet learned how to shave.

I've worn this life stitched from fear and obedience, forced onto me by hands that never asked. My sins hung off me. A coat that never fit right, constantly slipping, always dragging me down, as if the weight itself knew I didn't belong in this world.

I've seen things that should've split me open. Right down the fucking middle to my core. Things that tore through bone and left the pieces rattling inside me. Felt shit that still claws at my skin, feral and restless, waiting to pull me under. Dark memories. Hungry ghosts. All scratching at the edges of sleep, sinking their teeth in deep, reminding me I'll never outrun the monster my father made.

But with Emery, all that fucking noise just stills. All that's left is the steady rhythm of her breath against my chest. Soft. Calm. Real. She's not just the calm after the storm, she's the reason I even know what peace feels like.

And fuck, it's beautiful. The kind of beautiful that cracks me open. That makes my heart feel too small to hold it all. I was never built for this much feeling. Never meant to love this hard.

With her, I'm just Matteo. The boy who would burn the fucking world down just to keep her safe. To keep her right beside me. She makes me want something I've never fucking allowed myself to crave. Something that I would fight to have with my next breath.

I want to be worthy of the softness in her touch. I want to be worthy of the love she gives without hesitation, without asking for anything in return.

Sometimes, when it's just us, I let myself dream. That there's a world out there for us, somewhere beyond the blood-soaked streets. A place where we don't have to fight, where we don't have to bleed. Where the only scars we carry are the ones we choose to make.

In those stolen moments, I imagine it's just us, her heartbeat matching mine, our breaths tangled in a world that doesn't hurt. I fucking want it. More than I've wanted anything in my fucking life, but I know it's just a dream. And yet I can't stop reaching for it. I can't stop wanting it with every piece of me that's left unbroken.

"You're not like them," Emery whispers, her voice so soft it slides beneath the walls I've spent years building around myself.

"I don't want to be one of them," I mutter, voice raw, torn wide open. "I fucking hate it. Hate the monster they're making out of me."

The words burn going down, but they're the truth. I hate what they've carved into me, the blood, the brutality, the man I see when I look in the mirror.

Her eyes soften, and in that fleeting moment, I see the girl I fell for. The one who loved me when I was still broken, when I was nothing but shadows. The one who sees something other than the monster I've become. The one who still believes there's a future I can give her. A future we haven't lost to this fucking darkness.

"I know," she says, so simple, so gentle, it cracks something wide open inside me. "But you'll be okay. You'll find a way out, Matteo. I know you will."

And fuck, that's all I need to hear. Because in her eyes, I'm still worth fighting for. Even when I can't see it in myself. Even when I'm drowning in the lies I've been fed, she still believes in me.

I pull her tighter against me, clutching her like she's the last flicker of warmth left in a world gone dark. Right now, nothing else fucking matters but this. The girl I'd tear myself apart for. The girl I'll spend every breath trying, and probably failing, to shield from the nightmare we're both trapped inside.

My lips brush against her forehead, slow, lingering—an attempt to carve this moment into my bones. If I hold her soft enough, careful enough, maybe I can preserve just one piece of myself that hasn't been gutted by the violence. One piece that's still mine. Still hers. Still fucking human.

"I'll do everything I fucking can to keep you safe," I whisper, voice raw, cracked open, the words burning the whole way out. "I swear to you, Emery. I'll get us out."

But even as I say it, the lie curdles on my tongue. Because deep down, under every promise I give her, under every fucking hope I try to hold onto… I know the truth.

This life has already branded me. It's in my blood. Carved deeply into my bones. I'm the heir. The legacy. The next in line to wear the crown built out of blood and cruelty. That no amount of love could ever wash clean.

And as for my father… He'll never let me go. Not while I carry his name like a curse. Not while I'm the last thing he owns. Not while I still fucking breathe. The only way out for me is a bullet. Clean. Final. Merciful.

And maybe I'll welcome it when it comes. Because when the darkness finally drags me under… when it strips me of the last piece of whatever soul I've got left… I'll make sure Emery's nowhere fucking near it.

I'll push her away if I have too. Break her heart just to save her soul. Rip myself out of her life with my own bare hands. Because I'll be damned if Emery ever has to look me in the eye and see nothing staring back.

Chapter Fourteen

Matteo

The world outside is a vast expanse of nothingness. It's as if the night has swallowed the land whole, and everything in it.

The only light is the moon... bleeding pale silver over the tree-tops.

I sit in the chair, whisky burning a slow path down my throat. Eyes locked on the darkness outside. Hand hovering close enough to the gun on the table that it almost feels like control, even though I know it's not.

I haven't moved. Haven't blinked. Haven't fucking breathed properly in hours.

Every muscle in my body wound tight. Coiled with waiting, for the smallest twitch in the shadows. The tiniest breath of movement. The moment when silence breaks and the nightmare I was born into finally comes to collect.

Because I know they're coming. They always do. And this fucking silence is just the last mercy before the storm.

I should feel calm here. Safe. Hidden so deep in these fucking woods that even my demons lose their way trying to find me.

But nothing about tonight feels safe anymore.

Not with her scent still in my lungs. Not with the way my body still fucking aches for her.

Fuck, my head's a mess. A tangled storm of memories, mistakes, and she is at the center of every single one.

I can still feel her. Pressed tight against me. I can still hear the broken sound she made when I slid my cock inside her, like she was starving for me and I was the only thing left worth dying for.

She's burned herself into my brain. Every curve. Every breath. Every reckless surrender in the way she let me take her. She didn't just break me. She fucking destroyed me.

We fucked as if the world was burning down around us—nothing left to save but this. One last thing that felt real before the world catches up with us.

And even now... even sitting here with a gun at arm's reach and a death sentence crawling through the trees... it's not the fear that wrecks me. It's her.

I've never fucked that way. Not once. Not even close.

Not with the girls in the clubs, grinding on me to leave a mark, not because they want me, but because they crave the empire welded to my back. The name. The filthy, blood-soaked kingdom my father built on broken bodies and spilled guts.

They don't give a fuck about me. Just the crown. Just the cock that comes with the promise of power.

They drop to their knees fast, mouths wide open, not for me but the legacy. For the whispers they could spin after, eager to suck my cock just to brag about tasting the devil's son. How they wore my cum like a trophy.

The ones who spread their legs too easily. Their pussy wet not for me, but for the idea of what having my cock between their thighs could buy them. Leverage. Status.

Because it was never about the man behind the cock. It was about the empire between my legs.

None of them fucking mattered anyway.

They were just a way to get off. To take the edge off when this life, this name, this bloodstained legacy pushed too fucking hard. They were just a warm mouth. A wet pussy. A body I could use to forget for a few minutes. An easy, forgettable release.

None of them ever touched a single fucking thing inside me.

But her... Emery?

She didn't want the kingdom. She didn't want the blood. She didn't give a fuck about the empire or the legacy. She just wanted me.

And still today, she's the only thing that ever made me feel like I wasn't already six feet under.

Emery makes me feel everything.

None of them ever fucking touched that.

None of them ever made me feel like I was still human.

Every thrust. Every breath. Every broken sound that left her lips, it was a reminder.

Of how perfect she felt wrapped around my cock. Of how fucking dangerous it was to need anything this much. Of how easy it would be to forget everything I was born into, just to stay lost in her.

With her... it wasn't just fucking. It was freefall. It was salvation. It was home.

Her touch still lingers beneath my skin, burned deep into places I thought were already dead.

And no matter how far I run, no matter how deep I sink, it will always be her that I crave. It's always fucking her.

When I kissed her shoulder, it wasn't just a kiss. It was an apology sealed in skin. A silent fucking plea for forgiveness, for every fucked-up version of myself that's ever hurt her.

Because in that one fragile second, I was him again. The boy who used to slip through the shadows just to meet her beneath the stars. The boy who believed, naively, recklessly, that maybe we could outrun the blood in our veins. That maybe love could scream louder than legacy. That boy... The one who loved Emery with everything he had, like she was the only thing in this broken world worth saving. He's still here. Buried deep. Chained beneath the monster I've become. Trapped under the weight of every scar, every sin. He hasn't died. He's just been silenced.

Sometimes when she looks at me like she still sees him, I wonder if he's still clawing at the walls, begging for a way back to her.

She's still in me. In every ragged breath I take. In every fucked-up heartbeat I pretend doesn't hurt. She's carved into me. With the kind of love that scars and stays. The kind you can't drink away. The kind that stitches itself into your bones whether you want it there or not.

I bring the glass to my lips, the whisky burning dull and useless against the fire already crawling under my skin.

I feel her before I see her.

The way the air shifts. The way gravity tilts and points itself straight at her like it always fucking has. And then, she says my name.

One word. One sound.

"Matteo."

I close my eyes to savor it. Let it crawl into the cracks I pretend don't exist.

Every syllable, every whisper of breath. Her voice is low, soft, the kind of soft that fucks you up because it's too familiar. Too dangerous. It's my home wrapped in a sound I swore I'd never need again. And fuck... just hearing it, I already know that I'm not walking away from her this time.

When I open my eyes, I see her, moving across the room like a dream I'm scared to fucking wake from. She's wearing the sweat-shirt. The one I bought for her.

The sleeves swallow her hands. The hem brushes the tops of her thighs, hanging off her frame—too big, too soft. Too much of a reminder of safety I can't offer anymore. It fucking hurts, because it reminds me how she used to steal mine. How she'd pull it over her body just to breathe me in, as if my scent could shield her from the world.

Her hair's a mess, loose, wild, beautiful in the way chaos always is. Tangled from sleep, or from the way she runs her fingers through it when she's lost in thought... tugging, twisting, like if she pulls hard enough, the answers she's chasing will finally fall out.

It's the kind of mess I want to smooth out with my hands. The kind of mess I want to sink into just to feel her lean into me again. To pretend, for one fucking second, that nothing's broken beyond repair.

She moves toward me, barefoot, silent. But every step lands heavy against my ribs, beating through me like a war drum. Each one hits harder than the last because it's her.

Her eyes lock on mine, cutting past skin and scars, slicing straight into the wreckage I never managed to bury.

She has no idea what it costs me to meet her gaze and not fall the fuck apart. Or what it takes not to drag her into me and never let go.

She stops in front of me.

Close enough that I can feel her heat bleeding into the space between us. That every broken part of me aches to touch her. Close enough to wreck me, if she hasn't already.

And fuck, I want to pull her in.

Drag her onto my lap, claim every inch of her, because she is mine. Always has been.

I want to bury my face in her neck and breathe her in until there's nothing left of the world but the way she smells. I want to feel her. All soft curves and quiet strength pressed against me, grounding the hunger I live with every second of every day that I've survived without her.

I want to say something, but the words stick in my throat. If I let her in now, even for a second, I'll fall. And this time, there's no way back.

I look away. My jaw's clenched so hard my teeth might splinter. My heart slams against my ribs, furious, desperate to break free.

My fingers curl tighter around the glass. Whiskey scorches down my throat, pretending it can fix me. But it doesn't touch this. Doesn't touch her. Doesn't touch the wreckage she leaves behind just by looking at me.

My hands fucking ache to touch her. My mouth fucking itches to taste her again. To bite. To claim. But I can't move. I stay frozen, gripping the glass like it's the only thing keeping me from hauling her into my lap and showing her exactly how close to breaking I am.

She takes another step closer.

I feel her heat, her pull, like gravity's got her name carved into my fucking bones.

"Look at me," she says. Her voice slices right through every defense I still have left.

I don't move.

I can't let myself, because one look... one goddamn glance into those eyes and she'll have all of me again.

But Emery's never been patient. Never been the kind to wait for the pieces to fall neatly into her hands.

She moves in, and the ground shifts beneath me. Every step tears the fight straight out of my chest, one fucking breath at a time.

Her hand comes up, fingers curling around my jaw, forcing my head toward her, forcing my eyes to crash into hers.

And fuck... just that touch, just that heat against my skin, wrecks me harder than any bullet ever could.

My jaw tightens beneath her touch, every muscle in my body wound tight, coiled like a fucking wire stretched to its breaking point. My heart slams against my ribs as I meet her gaze, my resolve cracking wide open under the weight of her stare.

"I want to find my father," she says, voice splintering, a sound that slices straight through me.

It's more than pain. It's betrayal, confusion, desperation—all tangled and spilling out of her, a wound I can't fucking stitch closed.

"I want to know why he sold me out," she says.

I catch her hand and pull it away from my face, needing the distance the way a drowning man needs air. Because if she keeps touching me, I'll fucking break. And breaking? That's a luxury I can't afford anymore.

"No," I snarl. It's final. A slammed door she's not getting through.

"Why not?" she snaps, her eyes burning into mine like she's trying to tear the truth out of me with nothing but fury and hurt. "I have a right to know, Matteo."

She does. Fuck, I know she does. But some truths don't bring peace.

Some answers don't heal. They just hollow you out even deeper, leave you bleeding in places no one can fucking see.

I've already watched this world take enough out of her. Already seen it try to gut her and leave her with nothing but scars. I won't be the one to finish the job.

I throw back the rest of the whiskey, welcoming the burn, needing the distraction. Anything to keep me from drowning in the way she's looking at me.

Emery sees it for what it is. A dodge. A fucking diversion. It pisses her off, burns through her eyes like a slap I fucking deserve.

I see it in the hard set of her jaw, in the way her shoulders square, ready for war. And fuck, I know it's aimed at me. But I don't give her an answer. Not yet. Not when the truth will shatter more than just her. She's not going anywhere near that fucker. Not while I'm still breathing. Not with my father's silence crawling down my spine, heavy and cold, a loaded gun pressed to the back of my skull. Not until I know what the hell's about to crawl out of the dark and come for us.

Her eyes flash, and before I can even move, she fucking explodes.

"Fuck you, Matteo!" she snaps, her voice splintering, fury and heartbreak bleeding out in every word. "You don't get to make that choice. You don't get to sit there, drowning in whiskey and lies, pretending it's about protecting me while all you're really doing is keeping me locked in the fucking dark."

She steps back, breathing hard, her fists clenched so tight at her sides it looks like she's holding herself together by force.

"I'm going to find him," she says, louder now. "With or without you. I deserve to know why he threw me to the fucking wolves."

She turns away, as if being near me might tear her apart. Her footsteps hammer across the hardwood, each one louder, angrier, an attempt to outrun the silence I wrapped around us.

She stops at the far window, arms clamped tight across her chest, the only barrier between her and a full-body collapse.

Her back's to me, but I see it all. The rise and fall of her shoulders with every ragged breath. She's barely holding it in, fists clenched, jaw tight, bracing against the scream clawing its way up her throat.

She stares out the window, searching the sky for answers I won't give. Praying it'll say something I won't.

"You know what hurts the most?" she says, still facing the window, her voice frayed and low. "It's not that my father sold me out. It's that you turned out no better than him."

And fuck... my stomach twists so viciously it feels like something just tore loose inside me.

Then she turns. Slow. Shaking. And fuck... there they are. Tears, slipping down her cheeks in silence, dragging pieces of her with every drop. And it wrecks me, because I've never seen her cry.

Not Emery.

Not the girl who stared down the world and laughed. The one who once looked me dead in the eye and said tears were weakness. A fucking waste of strength.

Those tears are because of me and for the first time in years, something real slams through the numbness I've spent my whole life building.

She stands there for a second longer, eyes searching mine, like she's trying to find the version of me she used to believe in.

When she doesn't, her voice cuts through the silence. It's sharp enough to fucking slice me wide open.

"I can't do this, Matteo," she spits. "I can't rot away behind these walls like some prisoner you threw a leash on. This isn't living, Matteo. It's a slow fucking death."

Something inside me breaks, and I know there's no putting it back together.

"You think you can just fucking walk out of here?" I hiss, the words ragged, torn straight from the wreckage inside me. "The second you step one foot out that door, there's a bullet with your name on it. That's how this world fucking works, Emery."

Her jaw locks, fire flashing in her eyes, but she doesn't flinch. Not a fucking inch. She leans in, closer. Right in my face. Daring me to stop her.

"So what, Matteo?" she breathes, voice low, shaking, barely holding together. "You pulling the trigger? Or are you just gonna let someone else do it? Because I'll take my chances in the open before I rot in here, than be trapped and treated like I'm already six feet under."

She doesn't move. Just stands there, staring at me as if waiting for the words I can't fucking give her.

When all she gets is silence, she turns away.

"I'm done talking, Matteo," she says, voice low, every word sharp. "Do whatever the fuck you have to do."

She walks toward the door, shoulders squared, steps steady, like she's already made peace with whatever hell's waiting on the other side.

The kind of peace that tastes like gunmetal and finality. She'd take the bullet. No hesitation. Anything's better than one more day suffocating in the same air as me.

My glass hits the table with a hard CLINK as I slam it down. In seconds, I'm on my feet. My heart pounding, breath ragged, moving before I can think.

"Emery." Her name rips out of me, wrapped in a desperation I can't fucking bother to hide.

I don't even know why the fuck I'm chasing after her. There's no way she's walking out of here; every damn door in this place is under my control. She knows it. I know it. But none of that matters when every step she takes feels like she's dragging my heart across broken glass.

I catch her just as her fingers graze the door.

My arm wraps around her waist without thinking, fast, unrelenting, yanking her tight against my chest. Her breath stutters, but she doesn't move, doesn't speak. Just stands there, caught in the wreckage of what we are.

I grip her tighter, my mouth grazing her ear as I say, "If you think I'm gonna stand here and let you walk out there just to take a fucking bullet to the head, you're out of your goddamn mind."

She stiffens in my arms, but I pull her closer, locking her against my chest. My voice softens.

"I've seen what's waiting out there, Emery. I know exactly how fast this world chews up people like you and spits them out into a shallow grave."

She breathes slow, ragged, pulling herself back together one broken piece at a time.

Then she turns. Just enough to meet my gaze. And fuck... it hits hard. That look, cold, gutted, cuts through me. She's not just seeing me. She's seeing through me.

And I don't think there's anything left she wants to find.

"I need answers, Matteo," she says, her voice breaking. "I need to find my father. I need to hear the fucking truth from his mouth. Not yours. Not anyone else's." Her breath shudders, but she barrels on. "And if what you've said is true... if he really sold me out, then he's yours. Drag him back to your father. Use him. Break him. Do whatever fucked-up shit you have to do to end this nightmare." She pauses, pulling in a shaky breath. "But until I look him in the eyes and see it for myself, I'm not stopping. Lock me up. Chain me down. I'll tear this fucking place apart with my bare hands if I have to."

I stand there, arms still wrapped around her, her words echoing in my skull like fucking gunshots.

I let out a slow breath. My voice comes out rough, scraped raw over gravel. "Do you know where your father is?"

She doesn't hesitate. "Yes," she says, like the word's been sitting on her tongue for days, waiting for the right moment to cut loose. "I know where he is."

Fuck.

It hits me hard.

How fiercely she fought to protect him, even when I had her tied to that chair, breaking her down piece by brutal piece. She didn't bend. Didn't crack. Wouldn't give him up, no matter how hard I pushed. She carried his secrets in her veins, took every hit as if it belonged to her, endured the pain without flinching.

She's tough. I always knew that. But watching her survive that kind of hell? It rewired something in me. Because if she's willing to risk everything now, willing to hand me his location after everything I did to her, then I know one thing for fucking sure: nothing's going to stop her from facing him. Not me. Not fear. Not even the wreckage we left behind.

"Where is he?" I ask.

She doesn't flinch. Just lifts her chin, eyes locked on mine like she's daring me to look away.

"Promise me, Matteo," she says, and fuck, there's that fire in her voice. It's sharp. Wild. Untouched by everything the world tried to rip out of her. "Promise me that if I tell you, you won't twist it into some sick play to crawl back to your father. I want the truth. My truth. And I want a real fucking promise this time. Not another lie you use to spin, just one more of those lines you fed me back when you still knew how to pretend you gave a shit."

I turn her in my arms, dragging her flush against me, my breath hot against her face.

"You think after I put a bullet through Rocco's skull, I get to waltz back into my father's world as if nothing fucking happened?" I growl, voice rough, cracking at the edges. "You think this is some kind of fucking game?" I lean closer, my voice dropping, lower, darker, deadly. "We're both on his hit list, Emery. You and me. It doesn't matter what we do, doesn't matter how far we fucking run. He won't stop until we're both rotting six feet under." My grip tightens, breath shaking with the weight of it. "The only way we survive this shit... is together."

"Then fucking prove it," she snaps. "Because if I give you this... if I give you him...I need to know you're not gonna use it to save your own ass and damn me in the process." She moves closer, her voice low, furious. "I'm not your leverage. I'm not your pawn. I'm not another fucking casualty in your war."

Her words cut, straight to the bone. "You really think I'd sell you out to save my own fucking skin?" I snarl. "If I wanted to fuck you over, Emery, you'd be lying dead next to Rocco right now." I lean in closer, breath hot against her lips, every word a fucking warning. "Don't fucking push me."

Her eyes flare, fierce, wild, a spark of fury lighting up the room.

"Push you?" she retorts. "Fuck you, Matteo. How many promises did you break? How many times did you swear you'd protect me, only to feed me lie after fucking lie and shove me deeper into this hell?" Her chest heaves, her rage crackling like a live wire between us. "You don't get to stand there and act like you're some goddamn savior. Not after every bullshit promise you fed me just to keep me chained. So yeah...I fucking need proof. Because I'm done choking on your lies."

"I never fucking lied to you," I rasp, the words dragged raw from somewhere too deep to fix. "Not when it was shit that mattered. Not when it was about you."

Her laugh is sharp, bitter. No humor, just jagged hurt.

"Oh yeah?" she snaps, her chest brushes mine. "Tying me to a fucking chair was your version of trust, Matteo?" Her voice cracks, but she doesn't back down. Doesn't even blink. "That was you showing me how much I meant to you?"

She shoves the words between us like knives.

"So don't stand there and tell me you didn't fucking lie. Every promise you made to protect me, every word you whispered in the dark..." Her breath shakes, but her stare never wavers. "It all meant nothing the second you chose to fucking hurt me instead."

"I did it to protect you," I snarl, the words ripping out sharp, louder than I mean them to be. "You think pushing you away was easy? You think tying you to that fucking chair was some goddamn power trip? For fuck sake... it was me or them, Emery. You think I fucking wanted to do it? You think I enjoyed seeing you like that?" My eyes burn into hers, every muscle in my body strung so fucking tight I could snap. "I tied you to that chair because if I didn't... if I didn't make it look real, my father's men would've stepped in. And trust me they wouldn't have stopped. They would've torn you apart just to watch you fucking bleed." My voice drops, softer, the weight of it punching out of me. "I did it to protect you, Emery. To buy you time. To keep them from turning you into something you'd never fucking come back from."

I pause, jaw clenched, breath ragged.

"I chose the lesser evil," I say. "I chose me because at least with me, you had a fucking chance." My chest heaves, every muscle locked so tight it aches. "I kept you at arm's length when we were kids because I had to... Because dragging you deeper into my world would've eaten you alive." I suck in a breath that feels more like a wound. "And fuck, Emery... I couldn't watch that happen. Not to you. Not to the only good thing I ever fucking had."

She opens her mouth to fire back, but I cut her off before she can speak, the truth tearing from me before I can shove it back down.

"Because I fucking love you," I growl, the words breaking out of me, cracked and raw. "I did all of it because I love you. And I didn't know how to love you without fucking ruining you in the process."

She goes still.

Completely fucking still.

Her breath catches, like I just knocked the air out of her with nothing but words.

For a second, she just stands there, blinking at me, unsure if she actually heard me or if her mind's fucking with her again. Her eyes flicker. Shock, disbelief, pain... all crashing together in one brutal, beautiful moment. The fire in her dims, just for a heartbeat. The ground's split beneath her feet, and now she's got nowhere to fucking stand.

"You..." she whispers, barely audible more to herself than to me. Her brows knit. Her lips part, then press together again, caught between the urge to scream or collapse. But then her voice pushes through, low and shaking. "You don't get to say that," she says, head shaking, eyes shining with everything she's trying so damn hard to hold back.

"Not after everything. You don't get to say you love me... when everything you did screamed you fucking didn't."

I stare at her, at the way her chest heaves. At the way her jaw's clenched so tight it looks like it might snap.

But it's all out there now. No taking it back. The words I swore I'd never say. The truth I buried so fucking deep I thought it'd rot before it ever saw the light. But fuck it. If this ends tomorrow... if I step outside and get a fucking bullet like I'm goddamn waiting for, then at least I'll go down bleeding honest to her.

"I've loved you every fucking day, Emery," I growl, voice shaking, cracked wide open.

Her breath stutters, but I don't let up. I can't. Not when it's the only fucking thing left in me that's real.

"Even when I wanted to hate you," I rasp, the words ripping out ragged. "Even when I told myself you were better off without me. Even when I shoved you so fucking deep into the dark, thinking it was the only way to save you from the worst parts of me." My voice breaks, just long enough to bleed. "I loved you through all of it. Through the fucking silence. Through the violence. Through the goddamn wreckage of what I became."

I pause, breathing hard, my eyes locked on hers, the only thing anchoring me to this fucked-up world.

"I didn't say it to you back then because I thought loving you would fucking destroy you. And maybe it still will. But don't you fucking stand there and tell me it wasn't real. That every time I pushed you away, it was me trying like hell to save you... even when it fucking killed me."

She stands there.

Silent.

Eyes locked on mine like she's trying to see if this is another lie dressed in desperation, or if I really just ripped my fucking chest open and handed her everything I never had the guts to say.

The silence stretches. Tight. Frayed at the edges.

And then she speaks. Her voice is quiet when it comes.

"Then why didn't you fight for me?" she asks. "Why did you let me think I was nothing to you?" Her voice cracks, but her eyes don't waver. "I would've walked through fire for you, Matteo.

I fucking bled for you. And all I ever wanted—" she breaks off, swallowing down the ache, "was for you to stay. But you didn't. You fucking broke me... and left me to pick up the pieces alone." Her hands clench at her sides, fists trembling from the effort it takes to stay upright. "And now you stand here and tell me you love me as though those words could stitch together what you shattered." She laughs, jagged and bitter. "I don't even know what's worse... What you did to me... or the brutal truth that I still fucking love you, even now."

My chest locks up so hard it feels as if it's caving in, ribs folding inward, crushing me from the inside out. Because she just said it. The thing I've been dying for and dreading in the same goddamn breath. She still fucking loves me. After everything. After the lies. After the blood. After every scar I carved into her skin and her soul.

She still loves me.

It destroys me in a heartbeat. It tears through every wall I built to keep her out. Leaves me standing here, bleeding and desperate and hers.

"I never fucking stopped, Em," I rasp, voice shredded, raw, the words slipping out before I can even think. "Not for a fucking second."

"Never stopped... what, Matteo?" She asks.

"Loving you," I rasp, voice breaking around the words, stripped of every bit of armor I spent years building around myself.

I lift my hand and cup the side of her face. My thumb brushing softly over her cheekbone, like I'm scared she might disappear.

"I fucking tried, Em," I breathe, my forehead nearly touching hers. "God knows I tried to bury it. I tried to hate you. Tried to forget." My thumb trembles slightly against her skin, and I don't even care. "But it never went away. I mourned you every damn day. And I loved you the whole fucking time."

Her eyes shine, tears trembling at the edges, and fuck, my heart feels like it's about to tear itself apart inside my chest.

She leans into my touch. Her warmth bleeding into my palm like she's stitching me back together without even trying.

"I never stopped loving you either," she whispers.

And those four words tear through me harder than any blade, any bullet, any fucking thing this world has ever thrown at me. Because she never stopped. She never fucking stopped.

And for the first time in years... I don't feel alone. Not lost. Not hollow. Just a boy who's still in love with the only girl who ever fucking mattered to him.

Her eyes flick to my mouth. Just once. But that's enough. That one fucking look is all it takes to tear the last thread of restraint out of me.

My mouth crashes onto hers, rough, reckless, starving. There's no control left. No walls. No armor. Just raw, desperate hunger pouring out of me, pouring into her, like I can somehow fuse us back together with nothing but teeth and want.

My grip tightens on her jaw, angling her head back so I can take more. Claiming her the way I should've years ago. The way I dreamed about it every fucking night I had to survive without her.

She gasps into my mouth... and fuck, it's the sweetest goddamn sound I've ever heard. My other hand fists in her hair, yanking sharp, dragging her flush against me until there's no space left, no room to breathe, no room to fucking think.

She tastes of defiance. Of forgiveness. Of every fucked-up, beautiful thing I never thought I'd get back.

My tongue slides past her lips, stroking, teasing, demanding she yield and she does. She softens against me, like she's melting from the inside. A desperate little moan that tears the last shreds of control right out of my chest.

"You're fucking mine," I say against her mouth, the words harsh, possessive, savage as a brand. It's not a promise, it's a fucking fact.

She kisses me back harder, fiercer, her body arching into mine like she's been waiting years for this, for me to finally say it, to finally fucking mean it.

I growl low in my throat. The sound ripped out of me as I grip her thighs, hauling her up against me so fast she gasps. But she doesn't stop me. Fuck no. She locks her legs tight around my waist, grinding her heat against my cock until I'm one second away from losing every shred of control I'm hanging onto. She's not even naked yet, and I'm already so hard it's painful.

I spin us around without breaking the kiss, slamming her back against the nearest wall, needing her closer, needing her fucking everywhere.

Her fingers desperately claw into my shoulders. Her mouth still fused to mine like she's trying to crawl inside my skin.

And I'd let her.

I'd tear myself wide open if it meant she stayed there forever.

"Fuck, Emery," I say against her lips, my voice thick with every filthy, desperate thing I've been holding back. "You feel that?" I grind my cock up into her, hard and ruthless, making sure she fucking feels it. "That's what you fucking do to me."

She rolls her hips again, slow, filthy, a goddamn tease, grinding down on me with one purpose: to ruin me. To break me open right here, halfway up the goddamn staircase, and leave me begging at her feet.

Every step is its own kind of torture. Her heat pressed tight against me, her body grinding against my cock like she knows exactly how to break me. She's not teasing. She's claiming. Dragging that sweet, hot pussy over my cock with every slow grind, every breathless moan against my throat.

She's daring me. Promising me exactly what's waiting the second I get her flat on her back.

"You keep grinding that sweet pussy on me like that," I growl, voice rough enough to tear skin, "and I'm gonna fuck you right here on this goddamn staircase."

She moans, soft, desperate, needing it, aching for it.

And fuck... if she keeps moving against me, I just might.

Chapter Fifteen

EMERY

He doesn't stop. Doesn't slow. Just keeps moving. One heavy, brutal step after another, like there's only one destination and nothing, is gonna get in the fucking way.

The bedroom door flies open, crashing against the wall, and the second we're inside, he kicks it shut, hard.

Then I'm flying.

His hands grip my ass, lifting me off him just long enough to throw me down onto the bed.

The mattress jolts beneath me, and before I can suck in a breath, he's on me. Crawling up my body, covering me completely. His eyes are wild, dark with hunger, his jaw clenched like he's one second from losing control and fucking me senseless.

"You've got no fucking idea," he says, voice low and rough, "how many nights I dreamt about fucking you right here in this bed," he mutters, sliding his palm up my thigh. Burning a path straight to my core. "Every time I wrapped my hand around my cock, jerking it to the memory of you. It was you I'd think of. Your mouth, your moans, the way you used to beg me for more."

My breathing stutters, hips arching instinctively into his touch, desperate for him, for whatever filthy piece of him he's willing to give.

"I'm not stopping," he mutters against the sweatshirt at my stomach. "Not until you're dripping... shaking... mine in every filthy way." His hands slide up under the sweatshirt and then he stops.

A low, brutal snarl rips from his chest. It's deep, dark, pure fucking hunger.

His eyes snap up to mine, and there's nothing soft in them, just need.

"Fuck, Em," he mutters, almost to himself, like the realization just knocked the breath out of him. "You've been walking around all goddamn day with nothing on under this sweatshirt?"

I bite my lip, trying to hold it together, but it's useless. He's already shoving the fabric higher, exposing inch after inch of bare, trembling skin.

His gaze trails down my body—a fucking prayer etched slow into skin—and then he moves. Drops to his knees between my thighs as if it's where he's always belonged.

He grips my thighs, spreads them wide, exposing my soaked, aching pussy.

Then he dives in. Mouth buried deep, devouring me with no warning, no slow lead-up. Just raw, relentless fucking worship.

He licks me as if he's dying for a fix and I'm the only thing that can fucking save him. I moan, clawing at his hair, frantic, until he grabs my wrist, and slams it onto the bed, and holds it there, forcing me to take every brutal, wet stroke of his tongue.

His tongue fucks into me, slow, deep, obscene, and I'm already unraveling. My mind's gone, body trembling with every slick stroke.

He groans against my clit when I grind down on his face, the vibration shooting through me, dragging a broken moan straight from my throat.

"Matteo—"

His head snaps up. His eyes, dark, wild, fucking feral.

"No," he says. "You don't speak. You don't fucking move. You take it. Every goddamn thing I give you."

Then his mouth is on my clit again, hard, hungry, relentless. His hands lock around my hips, holding me down, forcing me to take every savage flick of his tongue like it's punishment and worship all at once.

"I'm not stopping, baby. Not until you come all over my face, screaming my fucking name so loud everyone will know who owns this pussy."

His tongue works me open as if he's claiming territory, slow, controlled strokes at first, savoring every inch.

Then deeper. Rougher. Caught between worshiping me and wrecking me.

And fuck, he's doing both.

He hooks his arms under my thighs and drags me down, pulling my pussy tight against his face like he's ready to drown, and fuck, he wants to.

And holy shit, he doesn't disappoint.

His mouth works every inch of me like I'm the only thing that's ever mattered. Every flick of his tongue wrings another twitch from my body, another desperate whimper from my throat.

His mouth sucks my clit. It's slow, controlled, cruel... drawn out with the kind of focus that says he's got all fucking night to unravel me, one pulse at a time. Then his tongue flicks my clit, faster. Rougher. Filthier. Until my hips are grinding into his face, chasing the pressure, the rhythm, the high I can't hold back.

The moans rip out of me, and still, he doesn't fucking stop.

He groans into me, each desperate sound I give feeding him, fueling the hunger he's barely keeping on a leash.

And then... fuck. He spits. Right on my clit. The hot slick of it makes me flinch, makes my thighs twitch around his head. Then his tongue is there, lapping it up slow, shameless, like he's licking cream off a spoon.

"God, fuck, Matteo," I pant, my hands clawing the sheets, hips bucking like I can't stop myself, because I fucking can't.

"Quiet," he growls, lifting his head just enough to speak, his mouth soaked in me, lips glistening like he's been drowning and wants to go under again. "You wanna scream?" he snarls. "You do it when you're coming all over my fucking face."

Then he's gone. No hesitation, just dives back in. His tongue flattens and drags through my folds, like he's imprinting himself with every stroke. I jolt, cry out, but it doesn't stop him.

Then his fingers slide inside me.

Two. Thick. His fingers curl just right, hitting a rhythm that feels carved from muscle memory, every stroke built to break me.

His tongue's still works me, circling, flicking, teasing. Never letting up and I can't stop moving. I'm grinding into his face, my body jerking, twitching, owned. I bite down on my lip, trying to stay quiet, but the cries still tear out, raw and messy.

"Oh fuck... fuck, yes," I gasp, voice breaking, wrecked beyond repair.

He smirks against my pussy, fully aware of the mess he's making of me. "You're so fucking wet," he says, every word dragging heat through my core, setting me alight.

His tongue moves faster with slick, hungry strokes that push me right to the edge. The orgasm builds hard and hot, curling up my spine until my thighs are shaking and I'm gripping the sheets like they're the only thing keeping me grounded.

He knows. Fuck, he always knows.

"That's it," he murmurs. "Give it to me. Soak my face."

And I do. I break apart with a cry, my whole body snapping tight, hips rolling helplessly as the pleasure hits hard and deep. But he doesn't stop. His mouth stays locked to me, tongue working every last pulse, every aftershock, until I'm gasping and twitching under him.

When he finally pulls back, his mouth is wet, chin dripping, eyes locked on mine like he's nowhere else in the world but here. With me. On me.

He wipes his mouth with the back of his hand, then climbs up my body, heat pouring off him in waves. There's nothing soft in the way he moves, there is only need.

His hand wraps around my jaw, it's rough but steady, tilting my face until all I see is him. And then he kisses me. Hard and messy, all tongue and teeth. He kisses me, mouth still coated in the mess he made of me—slow, filthy, full of intention. He wants me to taste it. Wants me to know exactly what he just claimed.

"You feel that?" he breathes against my mouth. "That's you. That's what you taste when you come for me."

His cock grinds against my soaked pussy, thick, dragging right where I'm still aching.

"Fuck," he mutters, pulling back just long enough to yank my sweatshirt over my head and toss it like it's nothing. He stares down at me, eyes hot, jaw tight, chest rising fast.

"Look at you," he says, voice thick with reverence, hunger poured into every syllable. "Laid out for me. Dripping. Shaking. All fucking mine."

His eyes drag over me like a physical touch, it's slow and greedy. He takes in my tits, then trails lower, zeroing in on my cunt as if nothing else exists. His breath stutters.

"I've wanted us for so fucking long," he says. "I've dreamed about us, Em." He grabs one thigh and yanks it high around his waist, then the other, spreading me wide open, leaving me exposed, throbbing, completely at his mercy. "Tell me," he says, grinding his cock against me so hard I gasp. "Tell me you want me to fuck you." Another grind. Deeper. Rougher. "Tell me you want this cock so far inside you, that you'll forget your own fucking name."

I meet his gaze, chest heaving, lips parted. "I want you, Matteo," I breathe, the words tumbling out like a prayer. "I want your cock. I want you inside me. Right fucking now."

That's it.

That's all it takes.

His eyes darken, something unhinged flashing through them before he tears off me, fingers jerking at his belt like it's strangling him. The second he gets it undone, his eyes drop, and he sees it. The soaked patch of wetness I left on his pants.

"Fuck," he mutters. "I should make you lick it off."

The threat hits, making my pussy clench so tight it aches.

He kicks off his pants, rips that expensive cotton shirt over his head, and fuck me he's lethal.

All cut muscle and chaos. Scars carved across his skin, battle lines etched deep. Dark ink coils over his chest, snakes down his abs in a perfect, filthy path that ends at his cock.

And fuck, that cock. Thick. Hard. Leaking.

The head slick with pre-cum, flushed and begging for my mouth.

He's beautiful in the dirtiest way possible. Every inch of him built to ruin me. My lungs forget how to work. All I want is to drop to the floor and choke on him until he's the only thing I can taste.

He fists his cock and strokes it slowly, putting on a show, knowing damn well I'm already dripping for it. His eyes stay locked between my legs, fixated on my pussy like it's the fucking prize he's been hunting for.

He steps closer, pressing the soaked head right against my entrance, dragging it through the mess I've made for him, slow, teasing glides that make my thighs tremble.

A crooked smirk cuts across his face as he drags it through my folds again, and again, until I'm squirming beneath him, begging without a single word.

"Look at you," he says. "So, fucking wet for this cock. You need it, don't you? Need me to stretch this sweet little pussy until you forget how to fucking think?"

I whimper. That's all he needs.

He thrusts... hard.

One brutal push that knocks the air from my lungs and tears a broken, desperate sound from my throat. No warning. No build-up. Just his cock forcing its way into my tight, greedy cunt... stretching me wide, making my eyes roll back.

"Fuck," he bites out, buried to the base, balls pressed flush to my skin. His fingers dig into my hips like he's trying to anchor himself. "This pussy was made for me. You were made for me."

My legs lock around his waist, desperate to keep him there, to keep him deep. His cock twitches inside me, thick and hard, like he's seconds from losing control.

"You feel that?" he breathes against my ear. "That's me right where I belong."

He pulls back slow, dragging every swollen inch out of me until only the tip remains, stretching the moment out, making me ache.

Then he slams back in with enough force to shake the fucking walls.

The headboard crashes against the wall with a crack, every thrust brutal, relentless—fucking the breath from my lungs and the thoughts clean out of my head.

"Say it," he demands, each word slams into me with a thrust that rocks me to the core as if he's fucking the truth straight out of my mouth. "Tell me this pussy belongs to me."

I cry out, back arching off the bed, every muscle drawn tight, nerves lit up like live wires. I can't think. Can't breathe. All I can do is feel.

"It's yours," I gasp, voice shattering. "Fuck, Matteo... this pussy's yours. All of it. All fucking yours."

He lets out a sound on the edge of breaking, my words throwing gasoline onto everything already burning inside him. And then he takes me harder. Deeper. Each thrust carving him into me, not just fucking, but branding.

His rhythm turns brutal, filthy, desperate. Every thrust crashes into that spot that makes me see stars, drives me up the mattress, makes me cry out with every drag of his cock. I'm shaking and he doesn't fucking stop.

"You've got no idea what you do to me," he pants, his mouth at my throat, his teeth grazing the skin there like he can't help himself. "Nothing comes close to the feel of your pussy wrapped around my cock."

Then he slams into me again, so hard the bed frame crashes into the wall, the sound swallowed by the broken moan he rips straight from my chest.

"You feel that?" he breathes, forehead pressed to mine, voice rough. "You're gripping me so tight. It's like this pussy knows exactly who it belongs to."

My body starts to unravel beneath him, every thrust pushing me closer to that edge.

Then his hand slides between us. His fingers find my clit with devastating precision, circling hard and fast, like he's chasing my release with everything he's got.

"Matteo... fuck—" I cry, hips jerking, pressure building fast and brutal. My body's strung so tight I can barely hold it in.

"Yeah, you're close," he says, eyes locked on mine, devouring every twitch, every sound I make. "Gonna come on my cock, baby? Gonna squeeze me so fucking tight I lose it inside you?"

My thighs start to tremble. My nails dig into his back.

"That's it," he says, voice rough and thick. "Come for me. Make a fucking mess. I want to feel this pussy milk every goddamn drop out of me."

And then I break.

My orgasm hits like a fucking explosion, ripping through me so fast, so hard, it knocks the breath out of my lungs.

I scream his name as my body convulses, my pussy clenching around his cock with desperate force, it's tight, frantic, soaking him in everything I've got.

And the sound he makes when I do... It's not a moan. It's not a groan. It's a fucking surrender.

He drives deeper. Faster. His hips crashing into mine with a pace so frantic, so fucking precise, it feels like he's trying to brand me from the inside out. Every thrust lands hard, claiming me with an intensity that steals the breath straight from my lungs.

This isn't just fucking. It's a goddamn possession.

His hand slides off my clit and glides up, fingers wrapping around my throat, not hard, just enough to feel the frantic beat of my pulse hammering beneath his palm. Enough to show me who I belong to.

His hips slam into mine again, and again, and again. Each time deeper. Rougher. Like he's trying to bury himself somewhere no one else will ever reach. Somewhere only he gets to live.

His cock hits so deep I swear he's fused to something in me that was always waiting for him.

"You want it, baby?" he says, voice shredded and tight. "You want me to fill this pussy up? Want me to come so deep you'll feel it for days?"

"Yes," I cry, the word torn from my throat as I clench around him, body electric and aching and ready to break all over again. "I want it, Matteo. Fucking give it to me. Fill me."

And he does.

With one brutal thrust, he slams so deep it feels like he's touching parts of me I didn't know existed. His cock jerks inside me, thick and pulsing, shooting hot as he spills deep into my body. I feel everything. Every twitch, every drop, every broken sound he loses into my skin.

But he doesn't stop.

He stays buried deep, grinding his hips with slow, deliberate strokes, making sure I take every last drop. Sealing it inside me, claiming me with every pulse.

My body trembles beneath him, every aftershock rolling through me while my thighs cling to his waist and my clit throbs, over sensitive and aching.

Our chests press together, slick with sweat, both of us panting like we just survived something violent and holy all at once.

And when I finally blink the haze from my eyes, he's there. Hovering over me. Gaze locked to mine. Still inside me, still fucking me, slow, careful.

He's not just fucking me anymore. He's looking at me. Really looking at me.

His eyes burn into mine, still wild and intense. But now there's something else. Something open. Something unspoken. Like he's laid every broken, bloodied part of himself bare and handed it to me without a word.

"You feel that?" he whispers, his thumb brushing across my cheek, treating me as if I'm something sacred. "This...right here... this is us."

I feel it in the way he's still moving inside me, like he's trying to hold the moment still. I feel it in the stretch of my body, the throb in my cunt, the sweat on my skin. I feel it in him. In everything he's not saying, but giving me anyway.

And for the first time, I see him. Not just the man who fucked me senseless. Not just the brutal hands and the savage cock and the need. I see the man beneath it all. The one who never thought he could give a piece of himself to anyone. But he just gave me everything.

The one who's been loving me in silence all along... even as the world twisted him into something he never asked to be.

"Matteo," I whisper, my voice shaking, stripped bare in away I never let anyone see.

He leans in, rests his forehead against mine. His cock still inside me.

"I fucking love you, Em," he breathes into my mouth. "Always have. Every second. Every breath. Even when I shouldn't."

My heart splits open. Because when I meet his eyes, it's not hunger staring back. Not anger. Not the violence he's been carrying like armor. It's him.

The man beneath all the wreckage. The one who's always been there, just waiting to be seen.

"I love you," I whisper back. Every wall gone. Every truth laid bare. "God help me, Matteo... I always have."

He kisses me, the only language he's ever been fluent in. His hips keep slowly rolling into me, each thrust a silent promise, the only way he knows how to hold me together.

And that's when I know.

This isn't about erasing the past.

This is about surviving it.

This is about choosing each other, when everything else has tried to tear us apart.

Because somehow, through every scar, every broken promise, every mistake... we're still here. Still breathing. Still us.

He stays buried in me, letting me feel him. Letting me feel safe. His forehead against mine, our chests rising and falling like we're one heartbeat.

Then slowly he moves. Pulls out of me, and the drag of his cock leaves me aching, empty, still wet and dripping.

"Look at you," he murmurs, eyes locked on the mess between my legs. "Fucking dripping with me. Just like you should be."

He leans in and kisses the curve of my stomach. Then lower. His mouth trailing over my skin until he's between my thighs again.

By the time he gets there, I'm already shaking, legs falling open on instinct, silently begging for whatever he's about to give me.

He spreads me wide and stares down at the wreck he made of me like he's fucking proud of it.

"You're not wasting a single drop," he says. Then he pushes two fingers deep into me, shoving his cum right back inside.

His fingers fuck into me with a rhythm that borders on filthy, his mouth locked on my clit, starving for me all over again.

"I want you to feel me inside you all night," he says against my skin, each word a pulse of heat straight to my core. "Want you fucking leaking with me. Smelling of me. Being mine."

When he finally pulls back, his lips are slick, fingers shining with the mess he's made of me. His cum. My cum. All of it.

Then he grins, dark, wicked, possessive as fuck and mutters, "Fuck it. I'll fill you again later."

Before I can even catch my breath, Matteo is already moving. He stands, then bends, scooping me into his arms like I weigh nothing.

He carries me across the room and kicks the bathroom door open with his foot, striding straight to the shower like a man on a mission. One twist of the knob and the water roars to life. It's hot, punishing, slamming against the tile as steam floods the space around us.

He steps under the spray with me still in his arms, no intention of letting go. The heat crashes over us, soaking into our skin. Water pours down in sheets, rinsing off the sweat, the cum, the mess he made of me.

Matteo sets me back down on my feet with a gentleness that doesn't match the way he just fucked me senseless. My legs wobble, but his arms are already there, wrapping around me like I'm something precious he's scared I'll shatter.

The steam swirls thick around us, wrapping us in heat, in something heavier and softer than either of us know what to do with.

Without a word, Matteo reaches for the body wash. I watch as he pours it into his hands, and starts to clean me. It's slow, caring, almost worshipful. His palms glide softly over my skin, over every bruise and mark he made, over every place he's claimed.

He doesn't rush it. He doesn't tease. Just touches me like he's trying to memorize what he broke and put back together all at once.

"Turn around," he whispers.

I move slowly, every muscle trembling as I turn for him.

His strong hands slide up to my shoulders, kneading deep, washing away the tension. When his fingers drift higher, threading into my hair, working shampoo through the strands, I close my eyes and lean back into him, letting myself feel it.

This is the Matteo I remember. The boy who used to brush my hair out of my face. The boy who would tell me I was beautiful when I felt like nothing but scars. The boy who loved me before the world taught him how to bleed.

His fingers glide through my hair, careful, almost reverent, rinsing the soap away with clean, steady passes. And then his mouth finds the back of my neck, lips pressing soft against my wet skin, and fuck... my heart thumps for him.

I turn back around, lifting my eyes to his... and then I see it. He loves me.

Even with everything he's been through. Even with all those scars on his soul. The cold, ruthless man he's become is still there, etched into every brutal line of him. But under it all, buried but still beating, is the boy who was always mine. The boy who still is.

Matteo lifts his hand and brushes my wet hair from my face, his fingers lingering, trembling a little—afraid to let go. His touch maps the shape of me, slow and reverent, as if he's trying to memorize every inch all over again.

"I should've never let you go," he says, voice rough and low, each word bleeding out of him as if it costs more than blood. "I thought... if I kept you away, I could protect you. But the truth is... I was just trying to protect myself."

I don't speak. Because I don't know what to say to that. All I see is the cracks in his armor. The guilt he's been dragging around, heavy as a fucking anchor. The way his hands still shake when they touch me. Not from lust this time, but from everything he's been swallowing down for years.

"I'm not that kid anymore," he says. "But fuck... when I'm with you... I feel like maybe there's still a piece of him left. The part you loved. The part that still fucking loves you."

I reach up, my hand sliding along the sharp line of his jaw. My thumb brushing against the rough stubble there. Holding him like he's something fragile.

"I never stopped looking for him," I whisper. "Even when you buried him. Even when you tried to make me hate you. I never fucking stopped."

He exhales hard, like my words punched straight into something he's been trying to bury for years.

Then he pulls me tighter, crushing me against him, his lips pressing to my temple, my cheek, my jaw. Soft desperate kisses, like he's trying to say all the things he still can't find the words for.

We stay that way, suspended in a moment that stretches on forever.

Us wrapped in steam, in heat, in each other. His fingers trail slowly down my spine. It's not sexual, just calming—his touch reverent, as though he's retracing something sacred he nearly lost. Every inch of me, memorized again, worshipped like a prayer he thought he'd never get to say twice.

He lifts my hand, presses a kiss to my knuckles, then lower, to my wrist, where my pulse thrums wild beneath his mouth.

"Let me take care of you now, Emery, " he murmurs, his voice a breath against my skin, a vow and a fucking plea all at once.

He reaches behind me and shuts off the water.

For a moment, we just stand there, dripping, shivering, breathing each other in.

Matteo snatches a towel off the rack and wraps it around me. Then he grabs another towel, barely drags it across his chest and arms before tossing it to the floor like he couldn't care less.

And just like that, he's on me again, closing the space—refusing to let distance exist between us, as if even air is too much separation.

His eyes lock onto mine. When he speaks, his voice is low, certain.

"If we do this, Em," he says, brushing the wet strands from my face with a touch so gentle it wrecks me all over again, "we do it together. No more fucking distance between us."

I blink up at him, and he continues, the words tearing out of him faster than he can stop them.

"I don't give a shit if we've only got a few days left or a few fucking hours," he says, voice rough, savage with emotion. "I'm choosing you, Emery. You." His hands frame my face, holding me steady. "If everything goes to shit tomorrow, I want to go down knowing I had you next to me. Fuck it all, Em," he snarls, voice cracking open. "Your father. My father. The blood. The fucking legacy. None of it fucking matters if I don't have you."

I press my forehead to his. My heart is pounding so loud, I swear he can feel it crashing against him.

"Then don't let me go this time, Matteo," I whisper, voice shaking. "Not like before."

His breath shudders against my mouth as he leans in, brushing his lips over mine. "I promise I won't," he breathes against me. "Not ever fucking again."

CHAPTER SIXTEEN

MATTEO

She is asleep next to me, naked, wrapped in the sheets, her face half-hidden in the pillow. Her breathing is slow, steady, like whatever war she's been fighting has finally gone silent. Her skin's still warm, lips slightly parted, hair a beautiful disaster, still wet, wild and perfect.

And fuck, she's so beautiful. It's almost cruel. Because now that I finally have her back, I realize just how easy it would be to lose her all over again.

I can't fucking lose her. I can't let that happen. I won't. Not this time.

Carefully, almost reverent, I brush my thumb along her cheek, memorizing the feel of her under my hand like I'm some fucking addict who knows his next hit might be his last.

She sighs quietly, shifting closer, instinctively seeking me out even in sleep, like some part of her needs me here.

Loving her fucking hurts. It always has. But knowing tomorrow might never come for us... that guts me. The second we step out of this house, it all slams into place—my father, hers, the blood between us, binding us in chains that threaten to tear us limb from fucking limb.

But tonight... Tonight, she's mine. And I swear to God, I'd burn the whole fucking world to ash before I let anyone lay a hand on her.

She shifts against me, it's just a small, sleepy movement, her hand drifting across my stomach.

She has no idea what she does to me. How the simple brush of her fingers calms the chaos. How she silences the storm without even trying.

My arm tightens, pulling her closer until her leg drapes over mine and her head fits perfectly into the curve of my neck, like it was made to be there. Maybe it always was. Maybe every fucked-up road, every wrong turn, every scar etched into me was just leading back to this moment. Back to her.

I press a kiss to her forehead, a vow etched into her skin, silent but deadly fucking clear.

If anyone comes for her, they don't walk away. I won't flinch. I've killed for less. And if it ends with a bullet in my skull? So be it. It will be worth it. As long as she's still breathing.

The sky outside is still dark, just that deep, ink-blue stretch before sunrise. The kind of silence that feels like the whole damn world is holding its breath.

I shift carefully, sliding out from under her, moving slowly, careful not to wake her.

She murmurs something soft, curling tighter around the pillow, and fuck I let myself look at her.

One more second. One more stolen breath of her before I drag myself away.

I grab a pair of sweats, yank them on, and head for the window. The cold air slamming into me harder than it should.

My phone sits on the nightstand where I left it. It's dark and silent, like it's daring me to pick it up.

I move to it, the screen lighting up under my hand, throwing sharp white against the dark.

I stare at it. Waiting. Dreading. And still there's fucking nothing.

No missed calls. No threats. No warnings. Just silence. And that fucking silence... it's louder than a goddamn gunshot.

Because I know my father. I know the way he works. Silence is a fucking loaded gun cocked behind your head. It's the pause before the bullet tears straight through your skull. It's psychological warfare.

He wants me watching shadows. Flinching at every creak in the floorboards. Questioning everyone I trust.

He wants me unsteady. Half-broken. Dangerous to myself before I ever become a threat to him.

He's planning. He's letting me stew in it until I make the next move. And when I do? He'll already be five steps ahead, smiling while he pulls the trigger.

Maybe I should just say fuck it and call him. Bite the bullet. Face the devil who made me and end this shit on my own terms.

A clean hit. A threat. A trade. Something. Because this...this slow, gnawing silence of not knowing... it gets under your skin and stays there, rotting you from the inside out.

"Matteo?"

Emery's voice breaks through the dark, soft and rough with sleep.

I shift slightly, still sitting on the edge of the bed, the phone clenched in my hand like a lifeline, or a weapon, depending on which way the night turns.

She stirs. The sheet slips lower as she moves, falling in soft folds at her waist, leaving her bare beneath the glow of dawn spilling through the curtains. Her skin catches the light, warm, flushed, impossibly soft and for a moment, I forget everything else.

She blinks up at me, eyes heavy with sleep, the edges of a dream still clinging to her.

And God... she's beautiful. Not just in that breath-stealing way, but in the kind that makes something deep in your chest fucking ache. My ribs pull tight, too tight—strained under the weight of her, of this moment. Of the silence in my head, where every ghost I've been running from suddenly goes still.

She pushes up onto one elbow, the slow movement makes her breasts sway, soft, effortless, unintentional and suddenly I can't look away.

I'm frozen, watching her—the picture of a man too far gone to fake control. Someone who surrendered long before he even realized he was falling.

"Is everything alright?" she asks, her voice a little clearer now.

God. She has no idea.

No idea how close I was to pressing that name on my screen, to setting everything in motion and watching it all burn.

No idea that it was her who pulled me back.

I toss the phone onto the nightstand. It hits the wood with a sharp crack, loud in the stillness, and she flinches, just barely, but I see it.

Guilt coils low in my stomach. I drag a hand over my face, trying to rub the tension from my skin, trying to find the right version of myself to give her.

I turn back to her. "Yeah," I say, the lie catching rough in my throat. "It's fine."

She doesn't believe me. Emery has always been able to see straight through my bullshit, cut through the lies, all the shit I tell myself to survive.

Her hand slides across the sheet, fingers brushing my thigh like she's trying to pull me back from whatever dark place I was about to let swallow me whole.

"Come back to bed," she whispers, voice soft but steady, eyes locked onto mine. "Come back to me."

And fuck... there's something in the way she says it. Like I belong there, with her. Not out there chasing the man who lit this hell inside me. Just here. Just her.

I crawl back in without a word, slipping under the sheet and dragging her into me like if I let go, she'll fucking vanish.

She tucks herself against my chest. Her fingers brushing over my ribs.

I hold her tight, because she's the only thing keeping me tethered to this fucked-up world. I breathe her in. Her warmth, her scent, the way her body molds against mine as if we were built to fit. My hand drifts down her back, tracing every soft line, committing her to memory all over again.

And for one reckless second, I let myself believe this might actually last. That somehow, against every fucked-up thing chasing us, we might still find a way to survive.

But it won't. Not unless we do something. Now.

I pull back just enough to see her face. To look into those sleepy, beautiful fucking eyes. The ones that still manage to see the best in me even when I'm drowning in the worst.

"We need to come up with a plan," I murmur, my voice low, threading into the dark between us. "No more waiting for them to show up. No more staying on the back foot, waiting to get fucked."

She blinks up at me, waking up a little more, the haze clearing from her gaze.

"We have to get out in front of this, Em," I say, brushing my thumb along her jaw, needing the contact, needing her to feel the weight of what I'm saying. "Control it before it controls us. Before he makes the next move and we're left scrambling to survive it."

She's fully awake now, her body going still against mine.

"If we wait," I add, tucking a strand of hair behind her ear, my fingers lingering against her skin, "he'll use it. Use you. Use me. He'll turn us into fucking pawns in a war we never asked to fight."

She's quiet for a moment, staring down at the sheets pooled around her waist like maybe the answers are written there if she just looks hard enough.

When she finally speaks, her voice is soft, uncertain. Not weak. Just wounded.

"I don't get it," she whispers. "Why would my father do that?"

I shift beside her, watching the way her brow furrows, the way her fingers twist the sheets like she's trying to hold onto something solid while everything else falls apart.

"He knew what your father was capable of, Matteo. He knew the second he gave me up, I'd either end up dead... or used. So what the fuck did he think was going to happen?"

I don't answer. I just let her speak. Because fuck, she deserves that.

Because if anyone's earned the right to tear this open, it's her.

"He sold me out to save his own skin," she says, voice harder now, sharper, the numbness finally cracking to show the rage underneath. "But what was the endgame? Did he really think your father was just gonna forgive him? Take the trade and let him walk free."

She looks up at me. Her eyes are shining, but they're fierce. Confused. Hurt.

"What did he think he was buying with my life, Matteo?" she asks, her voice cracking right down the middle.

"Time? Safety? Another chance to crawl back into your father's good books and pretend he hadn't fucking betrayed him?"

I reach for her hand, but she doesn't take it right away. Just stares at it first, then lifts her eyes to mine.

"I just want to know why," she breathes, slipping her hand into mine. "Why was I the sacrifice? Why not run? Why not fight? Why not anything but that?"

"Because he was a fucking coward," I say quietly. "Because when my father came looking for blood, yours didn't have the balls to bleed for what he caused. So he gave you up instead."

She flinches, just a small jerk of her shoulders. She nods, slowly, part of her already knew. Maybe she just needed someone else to rip the wound open and bleed the truth for her.

"I still want to hear it from him," she says, voice harder now. "I want to look him in the eyes. I want to hear him say it. Hear him admit what he fucking did. Hear him own it."

I see it. That fire, that rage in her. The betrayal carved so deep it'll never fully heal. She's not just chasing answers anymore. She's chasing closure. And she's ready to burn the whole fucking world down just to get it.

"I'll get you to him," I promise. "And when he finally tells you the truth, Em..." I reach up, my thumb brushing along the sharp line of her jaw—grounding her, grounding myself. "If you don't want him breathing after that..." I lean in closer. "I'll fucking end him for you."

I mean it.

Every goddamn word.

"Then we work out our plan," I add. "But not before you get all the fucking answers you deserve."

She lets the silence settle between us. Then I see the shift in her. The heartbreak twisting into something harder. Something sharper. That's the thing about Emery... she doesn't stay broken for long. She bleeds and then fucking burns.

She pulls the sheet tighter around her chest, and turns those fierce, wounded eyes back at me.

"If it's true," she says, voice razor-edged, "and by what you've told me, it fucking is..."

She swallows hard, jaw locking tight like she's holding herself together with nothing but stubborn rage.

"Then we need to come up with a plan. Because once I face him and hear it from his mouth... I want to know what he did, why he did it, and what the fuck he was hoping for. Then we decide what we do next to survive."

She's pissed off. Done being anyone's fucking pawn.

"I'm tired of waiting for someone else to make the next move," she snaps. "If your father wants to come for me, fine. If mine still thinks he's got a card left to play, let him fucking try. But I'm not walking blind into another ambush." She leans forward, voice hard as steel now. "We take control. We stay in control. Whatever it costs. We decide the next fucking move."

She's right. No more letting these fuckers choose the battlefield. It's time to take the fight to them.

I nod, my eyes never leaving hers. "Then we start now," I say. "No more looking over our shoulders. We hit first. We hit so fucking hard they'll never forget who they tried to fuck with."

She exhales, the weight of it all flashing across her face, but she doesn't back down.

"We end it," she says. "All of it. Starting with my father."

It's been days. Days of planning, fucking, and falling harder for her than I ever thought was possible.

We spend the time mapping out every move, every escape, every contingency, until we can recite it in our goddamn sleep. But mostly.... mostly we spend it tangled up in each other. Fucking like we're running out of time. Because shit, maybe we are.

Every moment I fall in love with her all over again. Harder this time. Deeper. In ways I don't even know are still fucking possible for me.

The way she moans my name as she comes apart around my cock, clawing at my back like she's trying to drag me deeper inside her.

The way her body fits against mine when we sit in front of the fire, her back pressed to my chest. My arms locked around her waist like I'll fucking kill anything that tries to take her from me.

The way her laughter slips out, soft, real, wraps around me, a goddamn life raft in the sea I've been drowning in for years.

I memorize it all. Every look. Every sound. Every goddamn inch of her. Because every second feels stolen. Every breath feels too fucking fragile. And if the world comes for us tomorrow, I'm going down with her name in my mouth and her body imprinted on my fucking soul.

But after days locked away, reality starts to creep back in. We're running low on supplies, which means stepping out.

Stepping back into a world that's been sharpening its fucking knives while we've been pretending we're untouchable.

I pull on my suit jacket, every muscle wound tight, like I'm already bracing for the war waiting on the other side of the door.

I glance over at Emery. She's curled up on the couch, knees tucked tight to her chest, her eyes wide and too fucking quiet.

She doesn't say anything. She doesn't have to. I see it all written across her face... Trust. Worry. Love. All twisted into one silent plea that wraps around my ribs and squeezes.

"I won't be long," I say, voice low, rougher than I mean it to be.

She nods, just once. But her eyes don't leave me. They hold me there. I can't just walk out like this.

I cross the room in two hard strides, grab her face in my hands, tilting her head up until she has no choice but to look at me.

My mouth finds hers, soft at first, then deeper, hungrier, desperate like if this is the last time, if shit goes sideways out there, at least she'll know exactly how much I fucking love her.

I pull back slowly, my thumb brushing over her bottom lip, memorizing the feel of her like a man about to walk into a war he might not walk back from.

"I love you," I murmur. "Don't ever fucking forget that."

She gives me a soft, sad little smile. "I won't," she says, her fingers brushing against mine. "Come back to me."

"Always," I promise.

I linger for a while just standing there. Watching her. Burning the image of her into my brain until I can find the courage to walk away.

Walk away from the only good thing in my fucked-up life.

The door clicks shut behind me, and the cold hits harder than I expect.

Not the air. The absence. The absence of her warmth, her breath against my skin, the quiet weight of her trust still wrapped around my chest like a second heartbeat.

I pass the car and head towards the truck, tucked away in the garage. My hand grips the gun tucked at the small of my back, second nature now. Violence in one hand. Purpose in the other. And fuck if I'm not ready to use both.

I slide into the driver's seat, the leather cold against my skin. The engine growls to life beneath my hands, low and rough, a sound that fits the way my blood's pounding in my veins.

I shift the truck into gear and roll forward. Leaving the garage behind. Leaving Emery behind.

The cabin fades in the rearview with every second, swallowed by trees and silence, but I still feel her eyes on my back. Still feel the ghost of her kiss lingering on my mouth. Still hear her voice echoing in my head. *Come back to me.*

I will. I fucking have to. For her. For us.

The road into town feels like a countdown. Every mile dragging me closer to the edge of something I can't undo. Time moves differently when you know the peace you had might not be waiting when you return.

Half an hour later, I park on a side street, engine idling for a second before I kill it.

The town's waking up fast. People cross streets with coffee cups in hand, school buses flash red, and horns blare in lazy frustration. A mom wrangles two kids into the back of her SUV, and a teenager skateboards past like the world doesn't even touch him.

It looks normal. Too fucking normal. Like a smile stretched over broken teeth.

They have no idea what's crawling underneath. No clue about the war simmering just beneath their feet. About the names whispered in bloody alleyways. The blood debts and betrayals that never fucking die.

I step out of the truck, the door clicking shut. Cold air hits my face, sharp and biting.

I drop my head, eyes low, moving through the space—blending in as much as someone wired with danger and scars can in a place that reeks of quiet lives and small talk.

Expensive suit. Crisp lines. The kind of thing that makes people look twice. The kind of thing that doesn't belong here.

I move through the store fast. Grabbing food, burner phones, bottled water and gloves. Nothing flashy. Nothing stupid.

I don't linger. Don't talk. Don't make eye contact.

But still... Something's off.

The old man behind the counter glances up at me once, then again, eyes narrowing, unsettled, trying to place whatever it is about me that doesn't sit right.

The girl near the exit pulls out her phone, fingers moving fast across the screen. Her eyes flick to me, then away, pretending it's nothing. But her body's tense, shoulders tight. She's already hit send. I can feel it.

And that weight settles in my gut. The kind that says the clock just started ticking faster.

I pay at the counter and step outside, bag in hand. That's when I fucking feel it.

The shift. The tension. The way the air thickens, charged and heavy—as if the street knows something I don't. As though I've just stepped into a game already in motion, the pieces moving long before I got here.

People move around me, slow and disconnected.

A mother drags her kid by the wrist, eyes forward. No one looks at me for too long.

A dog barks from somewhere behind a rusted fence. There's a delivery van parked down the block with no driver in sight. A guy across the street smokes without blinking, like he's watching something.

Maybe me. Maybe it's nothing. But it sure as fuck doesn't feel right.

I grip the bag tighter and head toward where I parked the truck, forcing myself to move steady. Not fast. Not paranoid. But every fucking nerve is screaming. This is how it starts. Right before the first blow lands.

And then... the sharp buzz of my phone.

A message.

I yank it from my pocket, thumb swiping the screen. My fucking stomach drops.

Rage detonates in my veins before I even finish reading:

King Prick: You think you can hide her forever, Matteo.

Shit. The words burn into my skull.

I spin slowly, scanning the street. Looking for every movement. Every shadow. Every corner.

This is how he works, quiet, surgical. You don't see him coming. You feel it first.

I search for the ripple of something off. A face I've seen before. A stance too straight. A presence too still.

And then I see them.

Hands in their pockets. Eyes sweeping the block. Slow. Calculated. Like they're taking inventory. Too alert. Too focused. Too familiar.

My father's men. There's no mistaking it.

Panic grabs me by the throat. I take a sharp step back and duck behind the bush at the edge of the store. The branches bite into my arms as I drop low. My pulse thunders in my ears, my breath quick and shallow.

They haven't seen me. Not yet. But they're watching. Waiting. And if they're here, out in the open like this, then it means one thing.

They know. About Emery. About the cabin. About everything.

Did I lead them to her? Did I just hand her over without even realizing it?

Fuck. I watch them carefully. They exchange a few quiet words, eyes still scanning, still searching.

One of them checks his watch. Nods to the other. Then they both turn and move down the street, slow, casual, with the kind of swagger that says they've got all the fucking time in the world. That says they already know exactly how this ends.

My blood goes cold. And the second they're out of sight, I'm moving. Fast.

I shoot out from behind the bush and sprint to the truck. Every nerve in my body on fire and screaming.

My hands shake as I wrench the door open, nearly dropping the bag.

I slide in behind the wheel, heart pounding so loud it drowns out the rest of the world. The engine growls to life, too loud, too slow. I slam my foot on the gas, tires shrieking as I tear out of the parking lot.

"Fuck," I choke, my throat closing tight around the word. Panic claws its way up my spine. "Emery." Her name leaves my mouth like a prayer I'm already too late to say.

I'm racing against the clock. Foot slammed down, the engine screaming under me. I blow past every red light, every speed limit, every warning. None of it fucking matters. The only thing that matters is getting back to her before they do.

Because if they touch her... If they even breathe near her...I'll salt the earth with their blood.

The roads blur around me as I tear through town. Every second slices across my skin—it's already too fucking late. My hands strangle the wheel, knuckles bone white.

I can't stop seeing her face. The way she looked at me this morning when I told her I'd be back soon. Trusting me. Believing in me. Counting on me.

The truck fishtails, gravel spitting and skidding behind me. I shove the gas harder, and harder, the tires screaming as I fly around the last curve, the woods closing in fast around me.

The cabin's close now. Minutes away. Maybe less if I keep pushing. And I fucking do.

Because I don't care if I wrap this truck around a tree. I'll crawl the rest of the goddamn way if I have to. Nothing is stopping me from getting to her.

Branches blur past the windows and then I see it,

Through the trees.

The cabin.

It's still.

Quiet. Too fucking quiet.

I check my phone—no breach alerts—but I've seen them hit other places without a single warning. Just slipped through like ghosts while everyone was asleep.

I kill the engine before I even hit the driveway, letting the truck coast, breath caught in my throat, eyes slicing through every inch of the clearing. Scanning for movement. For shadows. For them.

There's no vehicles. No sign of a break-in. But still it doesn't settle me. It makes the silence worse. Heavier. Like the calm before a bullet shatters glass.

Please. Fuck. Please be okay.

I get out, slam the door and run. My boots hammering the dirt, heart in my throat, gun already in my hand.

Every step crunches beneath me, loud as gunfire in my ears, as I tear up the porch, muscles strung so tight I might fucking snap.

The front door's still closed. No blood. No shattered glass. No signs of a struggle. And that's what makes it worse.

Because if they got in without a fight, it means they were careful. It means they were quiet and they planned this.

I press up to the door, back tight to the frame, and lower my breathing. My ear meets the wood.

Nothing. No footsteps. No voices. No fucking sound at all.

Just silence.

I press my thumb to the scanner and hold it there.

One beat. Two. Then a soft click as the lock disengages. I twist the handle slowly, dread curling in my gut over whatever the fuck's waiting on the other side.

I slip inside, gun drawn, heart hammering like it's trying to punch through my ribs. The door creaks closed behind me with a soft click.

I sweep the living room first. The fire's burned low in the hearth, barely glowing. The couch is empty. Nothing is out of place... and yet everything feels wrong.

I move fast, silent. Check the kitchen, There's no sign of movement. The hallway is clear. Each footstep hits like a countdown. I nudge open the bathroom door with my boot.

"Emery," I whisper.

No answer. I grip the gun tighter. My chest tightens, every muscle locked down as I cross the space toward the bedroom. My finger brushes the trigger, my mind already prepared for what I might see.

Then... movement.

I swing toward it, gun raised.

And then I see her. Emery. Standing in the doorway. Eyes wide. Barefoot. And fuck she's alive.

"Matteo?"

I freeze.

Breath locks in my lungs, blood roaring in my ears.

She's okay.

She's fucking okay.

Relief slams into me so hard my knees nearly give out. I lower the gun immediately. Shove it into the waistband of my pants. The metal bites into my spine. Then I close the distance in two fast steps.

I grab her face in my hands. I need to feel her, to know she's real. Then I pull her into my chest, bury my face in her neck, and hold her so fucking tight it feels like my body might snap in half.

"What's wrong?" she breathes, arms wrapping around me.

I don't answer right away. I can't. My hands are still shaking. My pulse is a fucking drumbeat of panic.

I finally pull back and cup her face in both hands. Her skin is warm. She's alive. And fuck, I nearly fall apart just from that.

"I thought—" My voice breaks, chest twisting hard. I swallow it down. Try again. "They know," I whisper. "My father's men. I saw them in town."

Her body goes still. The blood drains from her face as her fingers tighten around my wrists.

"They sent a message," I say quietly. "They're coming for us."

I don't look away. My hands stay on her. Steady. Like if I let go, we'll both fall apart.

"We don't have much time," I tell her.

And even though I see it. The flicker of fear in her eyes, the way her breath catches. She still nods.

CHAPTER SEVENTEEN

EMERY

The mid-morning sun cuts through the windshield. It's too bright, too harsh. Like the world doesn't care that everything's falling apart. That we're barely holding on.

Matteo grips the wheel, his jaw tight, his knuckles bone-white. His eyes are narrowed against the glare, but I can tell he isn't just focused on the road.

He hasn't said a word in minutes, but he doesn't need to. The tension rolling off him is loud enough.

We're heading toward the one place I never thought I'd go again. The safehouse. The one my father kept hidden, buried beneath a life built on secrets and survival. A place meant for escape. For hiding. For disappearing.

But we're not running. Not this time. We're going straight into the fire. Even if it tears everything apart. Even if it breaks what's left of us to do it.

I glance over at Matteo. At the tension carved into every inch of him. The way his shoulders stay rigid, like if he lets them drop even a little, the whole damn world might collapse with them.

He's trying to hide it. Trying to stay steady. But I see it. Clear as day. Fear.

Not for himself. Matteo would walk into fire without flinching if it meant keeping someone else safe. But this... This is different. He's scared for me.

That hits harder than anything else has. Because Matteo's always been the strongest man I know. Ruthless. Unshakeable. The kind of man who stares death in the face and doesn't fucking blink. But right now, the cracks are showing.

He shifts in his seat, and his eyes flick to the rearview mirror. Quick. Sharp. Like he's expecting death to be following us in the next car back.

I reach across the console, my hand hovering for a beat before I touch him. My fingers graze the inside of his wrist. It's light, careful, like I'm afraid I might spook him.

And all the while, the thought gnaws at me... should I tell him... about what I've got hidden, the secret I've been holding onto like a loaded gun tucked behind my spine. My last card to play if everything goes to shit.

It's not that I don't trust him. I do. With everything.

But I also know how he is when it comes to protecting me. How far he'd go, how much he'd destroy. And if he knew what I was carrying... if he knew what I was capable of.

Would it calm him? Or would it break him?

He flinches, just a fraction. Barely there. But still I feel it. The tension thrumming under his skin. The way he's holding himself together with nothing but raw willpower and grit.

I slide my hand beneath his, threading our fingers together. He squeezes my hand hard, like he's trying to hold on to something solid. Something he's terrified of losing.

"We'll be okay," I say, my voice soft, shaking.

He doesn't answer. Doesn't even look at me. Just keeps his eyes locked on the road like it's the only thing that matters. His jaw clenches tighter, and for a second I wonder if he even heard me. But then his thumb moves slowly. A soft brush across my knuckles. A thank you. A promise. Maybe even a plea.

Because whatever the hell we're driving toward, whatever nightmare waits at the end of this road, I know we'll face it together.

The road winds through the backcountry like it's trying to lead us off the edge of the world. It's narrow, framed by tall pine trees that press in close on either side. The kind of road that disappears if you blink too long. The kind that forgets you the second you leave it.

Dust curls in the vehicle's wake, catching the light in hazy, smoke-thin ribbons. Sunlight fractures through the canopy in sharp beams. The air hangs heavy and still, watchful, an unspoken warning in the trees, as if the forest itself knows where we're headed and wants us gone.

We pass a rusted fence half-swallowed by vines. A mailbox leaning sideways on a splintered post. The deeper we go, the more it feels like stepping into a place time has given up on. Abandoned. Forgotten. But not by me.

I know these woods. I know the way they breathe. The way the wind curls low through the underbrush and carries the sound of your footsteps farther than it should.

I know the gravel turn off that disappears behind a thicket of trees, the one most people miss unless they've been taught to look for it. I know the shape of the land. The dip in the road before the final bend. The narrow trail that leads to a porch I stood on too many times, wishing it would collapse beneath me.

Matteo doesn't know this place.

But I do, all too well. This is where the lies started. Where the man who raised me became someone else. Where the past still lingers. And now we're heading straight into it. Not to hide. Not to run. But to finally face what's waiting there for us. No matter what it takes.

A rundown house outside of Millstone. Tucked between dying farms and long-forgotten backroads. Where the gravel turns to dust and the silence hangs heavy.

I can still picture it. The peeling white paint. A collapsed fence out front. One shutter always hanging loose, banging when the wind picked up. A place that always felt more like a hiding spot than a home.

My father used to call it "quiet enough to disappear, close enough to stay informed." He said it like it was a strategy, a rule, not a life. It was his backup plan. The fallback he drilled into me like muscle memory when I was too young to understand what survival really meant.

If things ever go bad, you come here. This is where I'll be.

And now, things aren't just bad. They're totally fucked, all because of him.

"It's about an hour out from here," I say, eyes fixed on the blur of trees outside the window. "Near the train yard past Millstone. Off a gravel road with the rusted-out grain silo. You won't see the driveway until you're practically on top of it."

Matteo glances over.

I pause, swallowing hard. "He used it as a safehouse...years ago." I drag in a breath, steadying the shake in my voice. "I don't think he ever stopped."

Matteo nods once, his jaw flexing.

"Why there?" He asks.

"Because it's isolated," I say. "And, because he thinks I'm dead." My throat tightens as I stare at him. "He'd be using it now not expecting me to show up."

A muscle ticks in Matteo's jaw. He doesn't speak, but he doesn't have to. I can feel it rolling off him in waves. Rage. Restraint. The kind of fury that simmers low, waiting for something to burn.

His whole body's strung so tight he's practically vibrating beneath the surface. Every breath's a war, controlled, barely holding back something brutal.

"He thinks I'm just a memory now," I say, my voice steady, but I feel the crack beneath it. "I was just another mess he buried to save his own skin. That's why he'll let his guard down. He won't see me coming."

Matteo looks at me for just a second, but that's all it takes. It's not just anger I see on his beautiful face. It's heartbreak. It's grief for everything he couldn't protect. It's rage at a world that let it happen. And underneath it all it's love. Fierce and fucking lethal. The kind that doesn't back down. The kind that kills to keep you breathing.

And I know if my father so much as looks at me the wrong way...If he breathes the wrong fucking word, Matteo won't hesitate. He won't ask questions. He'll put a bullet between his eyes and paint the walls with his fucking blood. Because that's what love looks like in this world we've grown up in. When it's been pushed too far. When it's been broken, tested, and still refuses to fucking die.

We have been driving for nearly an hour. Every passing minute, the weight in my chest grows heavier. Not just from where we are going, but from what I'm about to do.

Because I know this isn't just about finding my father. It's about facing the man who broke me before I even knew I was breakable. It's about walking back into a version of myself I tried to bury so long ago.

I press my palm to my thigh, trying to stop the shake in my fingers, but it doesn't help. The closer we get, the more my body remembers what it felt like to belong to someone who only loved me when it was convenient. To be a daughter and a liability in the same breath.

I can't stop thinking about what happens next.

What I'll say, what he'll do. Or what Matteo will do. Because I've seen what he becomes. And I'm not sure if I'm leading him into a conversation or a war.

He hasn't let go of my hand once. His grip is steady, solid in a way that should comfort. But I can't stop wondering if he can feel it. The tremble in my fingers. The way my pulse keeps skipping like it's trying to outrun what's ahead.

The road starts to curve. The trees start to shift. A subtle change, but I feel it in my chest. Like my body recognizes this place before my eyes do.

The branches hang lower. The air feels still. Like the forest itself is holding its breath.

I know we're close. Too close.

And no matter how tightly I hold Matteo's hand, I don't know if it's enough to keep me from coming undone.

I hold my breath the second the laneway comes into view up ahead. There it is, that goddamn silo. Rusted to shit, slouched like it's been waiting years to finally collapse in on itself. Half-swallowed by brush, forgotten by time. But still I remember it.

And just beyond it, far into the distance, barely visible through the snarl of overgrowth I see it.

The house.

His fucking safehouse.

Small and sun-bleached. Tilted, ready to sink into the earth and vanish. Tucked so deep in the trees, it looks half-swallowed already. A place where the lies always outnumbered the furniture.

"That's it," I mutter, my voice tight.

Matteo doesn't speak. He just pulls onto the dirt track, calm as sin, driving with the kind of focus that says he's done this a thousand times. Built for this kind of quiet war. Born in it. Raised by it.

A little ways down, he veers the truck off the path, tires crunching softly as he eases us into a dip behind a line of thick trees. Out of sight. Invisible. The kind of hiding spot you don't find unless someone tells you where the bodies are buried.

He kills the engine.

And the silence. It hits like a punch. Swallows us whole. No music. No voices. Just the low thrum of adrenaline and the deafening quiet of too fucking late to turn back now.

We don't speak. Just sit there, like if we move too fast, the whole thing might blow wide open.

Matteo leans forward, his movements precise as he grabs the binoculars from beneath the seat. He angles them toward the clearing, his eyes narrowing as he takes in the scene.

"Front door is shut," he mutters, voice low, focused. "Curtains drawn. One truck behind the shed." He scans the perimeter. "No guards. No lookouts. No posted men. If he's got anyone, they're inside." Matteo doesn't move, doesn't look away from the binoculars, he's waiting for the next piece of the puzzle to click into place.

I nod, throat dry, the weight of it all pressing on me. "He really doesn't think anyone's coming."

Matteo drops the binoculars into his lap. His eyes flicker with something dark, a mix of anger and disgust.

"Especially not you," he says. "He buried you the second he gave you up. And he sure as fuck never thought you'd come back from the dead to knock on his fucking door." He lets out a long breath. "If you don't want to go in there," he says facing me, his voice low. "I'll do it myself. I'll walk through that door, and I'll put a bullet in the fucker's head before he even gets a word out. No hesitation. I'll end it, Em. If you want me to."

He's not asking because he doubts me. He's asking because he wants to carry it for me. All of it.

I stare at him, at the man who's been to hell and still wants to stand between me and the flames.

"I need to do this, Matteo," I say. "I need to do it for me."

He nods. "Then let's end it."

We exit the truck in silence, the doors clicking shut behind us.

Matteo checks the gun on his lower back. It's quick, practiced, then he falls into step beside me. He's close enough to protect me.

We can't take the road. That'd be suicide. Especially if my father has eyes on the property.

So we cut through the scrub. Through the overgrown bushland, wild with bramble and sharp-edged branches, thick enough to tear skin if you're not careful.

It's slow, brutal work. Branches whip at my arms. Thorns claw at my jeans. But we push forward anyway, because there's no other way in. Not if we want the element of surprise.

Matteo follows close behind me, one hand on his weapon, the other steadying me anytime the path dips or roots try to pull me down. He doesn't speak. He's just there. A shadow at my back. A shield I never asked for but can't breathe without. Silent and deadly, keeping his body between mine and any threat that might be waiting in the trees.

Every step is a calculated move. Every pause, every crouch, every low breath is another piece of a silent strategy.

We just move.

The scent hits me before the house comes into view—gasoline and pine, soaked into the air like it never left. It makes my steps falter for half a second before Matteo's hand presses gently to my back, keeping me grounded. Keeping me moving.

Then, through a gap in the brush, I see it.

The warped siding. The gutter barely clinging to the edge of the roof. And the front window still boarded up from the inside. That board's been there for years. Splintered and sun-bleached, nailed in unevenly after I smashed the glass with a tire iron the night he locked me out.

It all looks the same. But I'm not.

This isn't a homecoming. It's a reckoning.

The house gives off exactly the vibe it's supposed to. That no one lives here. That no one ever will. Abandoned. Untouched. A perfect fucking decoy.

It's all weathered paint and warped wood. The porch sags just enough to scream stay the fuck out.

Because the outside... That's the lie. The real truth waits inside.

I remember it. The polished hardwood floors that gleamed under recessed lighting. The clean line, cold steel. Marble countertops and modern appliances that looked like they'd been pulled from a catalogue. It's modern. Immaculate.

I take in a deep breath, trying to pull myself together when every nerve in my body is screaming that I'm walking straight into the fire.

And then we move.

Fast.

The clearing yawns out in front of me, a goddamn graveyard, wide, exposed, and begging for blood. Sunlight slashes through the trees in harsh, unforgiving beams. It's too fucking bright, casting a spotlight on our backs, daring someone to take the shot. Out here we're targets. No cover. No shadows. Just two fucked-up souls marching toward the past, demanding something it was never willing to give.

Dust kicks up around my boots as we cross it, and all I can think about is how much blood this dirt has already buried. How much more it's probably about to drink.

Matteo's right behind me, silent, solid, dangerous as hell. I don't need to look to know he's ready to kill for me. I feel it in the way his steps echo mine, in the way his presence wraps around me, an invisible shield. If shit goes sideways, he's not dodging the bullets. He's catching them.

We hit the edge of the porch fast. I climb the steps, one by one, and the boards creak under my weight—long, aching groans like the house is waking up.

The front door looms in front of me, still and shut, but it hums with something dark beneath the wood, maybe something dangerous waiting on the other side of this door.

I stop just short of touching it. My fingers twitch—caught between knocking, breaking, or setting the whole damn thing on fire. My chest aches, straining to contain every fucked-up memory clawing its way up from the dark. And in that moment, every step I've taken since I bolted from this life starts crawling up my spine.

A scream buried years ago, still lodged in my bones, still humming under my skin.

Matteo's there. Close enough to catch me if I break. Steady and coiled, like a storm dressed in calm. He's ready to fucking react. To explode. To protect. To kill. All of it... just waiting beneath his skin. He's watching everything. Reading the shadows, ready to fuck up anything that breathes wrong. If this door opens wrong, he'll tear the whole fucking house down.

Nothing stirs behind the drawn curtains. No voices. No movement. Just stillness thick enough to drown in.

"Em... let me go first," he says, voice low.

I shake my head before he finishes. "No," I say, voice low but sure. "I want this."

Not because I don't trust him to protect me. Fuck, he'd take a bullet before I even saw the barrel.

But this... This is mine. It doesn't belong to him. It belongs to me.

My fingers wrap around the handle, and it jolts through me—a live wire under my skin. Cold. Charged. Wrong in every fucking way. My heart slams against my ribs, a frantic rhythm that screams at me to turn back.

But I don't. Because this... This moment is mine. Even if it guts me.

I stay there, holding my breath, somewhere between the girl I was before all this happened and the woman standing here now, trembling just enough for me to feel it, hate it, try to hide it.

Matteo watches, and he waits. One hand rests on his gun, calm but ready. The other... Probably just waiting to catch me if I fall apart.

I push open the door, and step inside.

The air feels different here. Stiff, sterile. The smell of polished wood and something faintly chemical fills my lungs, making my stomach tighten.

Every movement is slow, deliberate, as if I'm waiting for the floor to crack beneath me, for the walls to close in and suffocate me.

"Stay behind me," Matteo mutters, his voice low, as he steps in front of me, watching everything, protecting me like it's the only thing that matters.

I can't stop the shiver that runs through me as he leads me inside. The cold, polished beauty of the place. It's too perfect. Too clean. A place that feels like it was designed to be looked at, not lived in.

The floors are smooth, gleaming under the soft lighting. The walls are a mix of sleek, dark wood panels and glossy, white surfaces that reflect the light like it's something precious. The furniture is sparse, minimalist. Neutral tones. Grays, whites, and blacks.

There's no warmth here. No personal touches. Nothing that feels human. Just cold, perfect emptiness. The art on the walls is modern, and abstract.

I can feel the shift in Matteo before he even moves. His breath changes, deeper, measured. His stance shifts like a switch has been flipped. All soldier, all instinct.

We move through the first room; the silence surrounds us. The kitchen looks used, but it is empty. Cabinets left half-open. Dishes still in the sink. The place feels... abandoned, but not by choice. The house feels hollow now. The servants have vanished, and the life it held has slipped through the cracks, lost to time. Now, it's just him, left to do everything himself.

Then as we move forward, I see him, just beyond the narrow entryway, past the hallway leading to the back den.

My father.

He's sitting in an old armchair, facing the window. One leg casually crossed over the other, the cigar smoldering between his fingers, its smoke curling toward the ceiling in slow, lazy spirals. And there beside him, resting on the arm of the chair, just out of reach is a gun.

He's sitting there, watching the main road, unmoving, like a fucking statue—completely unaware that we've come through the back, that we've already breached the perimeter, already standing behind him, ready to strike.

Matteo moves first, just a fraction, a controlled shift, his hand shooting out behind him. His palm is open in a silent command.

Halt.

I obey, heart hammering in my chest, eyes locked on my father as Matteo takes slow, deliberate steps forward. Every movement is quiet, controlled. But beneath that calm, I can feel the rage in him, like it's boiling under the surface, ready to tear through everything.

The floorboard creaks beneath Matteo's boot. It's soft, barely audible, but it's enough.

My father flinches, his head snapping to the sound. In an instant, his hand shoots toward the gun resting on the arm of the chair, years of instinct kicking in like it's second nature.

But Matteo's faster. Way fucking faster.

Before my father even knows what's happening, Matteo is there, arm extended, the barrel of his gun pressed hard against the back of my father's head. I can see the tension in the way Matteo holds his gun like it's an extension of himself. I've never seen him more alive. More lethal.

"Don't," Matteo growls, his voice low, and dangerous. "Don't even fucking think about it."

Matteo's eyes are cold as he watches my father's every breath, every twitch.

My father freezes. Fingers hovering inches from the grip of his gun. Breath shallow. Eyes wide. Lips parted like he's trying to speak but choking on the truth instead.

"Matteo," he rasps, voice torn and brittle, scorched from choking on his own sins for far too long.

"I said don't," Matteo snaps.

He presses the barrel harder against his head, while his other hand rips the weapon from the chair beside him and hurls it across the room. It hits the floor with a brutal clunk and skids across the hardwood, spinning out like it's trying to escape the moment.

"You fucking move again," Matteo says, voice low, dark, vibrating with threat, "and I'll fucking drop you where you sit." His eyes narrow, venom bleeding into every word. "Try me. Blink the wrong fucking way, and I'll paint the walls with your blood."

His gun stays steady, perfectly still. But every inch of Matteo's body is locked and coiled like a soldier one heartbeat away from firing.

And then he glances at me. It's permission. It's power. It's mine.

That look says it all. This is your war, Em. Say the word, and I'll end it. One bullet. One breath. One fuck-you goodbye.

I move forward slowly, my boots striking the floorboards with a dull thud. Steady and final, like they're marking the beat to his unraveling.

With every inch I close between us, I watch it hit him. Then I see that flicker of recognition. That slow, creeping horror.

His body stiffens.

The cigar slips from his fingers, hitting the wood with a soft hiss as the ember dies, just like the fire he thought he still had left.

He stares at me as if he's seen a ghost. As if I clawed my way out of the grave he dug with his own hands. As if I've come back for blood.

And maybe I fucking have.

I tilt my head, just slightly. Let my lips curl, not into a smile, but something colder. Crueler. A quiet little fuck-you dressed as charm.

"What's the matter?" I say, voice sharp. "Didn't expect me to still be breathing, Father?"

He doesn't speak.

Doesn't even blink.

So I step closer, the words burning in my chest, aching to get out.

"I mean, you sold me out for what? Freedom that you'll never fucking get. Or did you really think that once he killed me, you were off the hook?"

His throat bobs as he swallows. Finally, he finds his voice, but it's weak, shaky. "Emery…"

I cut him off with a scoff.

"No," I snap, bitterness slicing through every word. "You don't get to say my name that way—don't get to act like it still fucking means something. You lost that right the second you gave me up to save your own miserable life."

Matteo shifts, his body still as stone. He's watching him, eyes cold, gun still raised. His finger rests on the trigger, but he doesn't move.

My father's voice is low, cracking, straining at the seams. "You don't understand what it was."

"I understand perfectly," I spit, cutting through his bullshit. "You had a choice. You chose you. You let them take me."

I stare down at the man who used to mean something. The man who once looked me in the eye and preached loyalty as if it were gospel. As if it were law. And then shattered it, shattered me the second it cost him more than comfort.

"Tell me why," I bite out, my voice shaking. Not from fear, not from grief, but from the white-hot rage clawing up my throat. "Tell me why your own fucking daughter became nothing more than collateral damage."

His eyes flinch away from mine. Coward. Like he can't stand the reflection of what he did staring back at him.

"Because it was you or me, Emery," he rasps, voice brittle and pathetic. "Because your name bought me another day."

I step closer. "Why? Was I just a name you could carve off your family tree to save your own fucking skin?"

He swallows hard, face paling beneath the weight of it all. The guilt, the fear, the truth he can't outrun. But he doesn't answer. He doesn't even try.

So Matteo steps in, fast and brutal. He shoves the barrel harder against his skull, forcing his head forward with a crack of bone-on-metal.

"Fucking answer her," he growls, voice laced with violence. "Or I swear to God, I'll make you choke on the truth myself."

His finger twitches on the trigger. It's not a bluff. It's not a threat, it's a fucking promise.

My father watches me for a second, then swallows hard, guilt crawling up his throat like it's choking him from the inside out.

"Because I thought you'd survive longer than me," he finally chokes, the words brittle, jagged. "Matteo's father, he doesn't just kill, Emery. He breaks. He dismantles people piece by fucking piece. But it's slow. Precise. Personal." His voice splinters, cracking under the weight of his own cowardice. "I knew what he'd do to me. But you..." He shakes his head, like that somehow makes this better. "I thought you'd buy me time."

I let out a laugh, it's bitter, harsh, cracked open at the edges. It tastes like blood in my throat.

"You thought Alessandro De Luca would spare me?" I step closer, eyes locked on his, burning with every fucked-up memory he handed me. "That he would dig through all that rot and suddenly find a fucking conscience? That a man who kills for fun would give me mercy?" My voice drops. "No. You didn't think I'd survive." I pause, just long enough for the truth to sink in. "You just hoped I'd die quietly."

"No," he admits, voice splintering beneath the strain. Desperation leaks through the cracks, ugly and pathetic. "I knew he'd hurt you. I did. But I gambled. I thought... I thought your connection to Matteo would be enough. I knew you meant something to him." He swallows hard. "I figured he'd step in before it went too far. That his father wouldn't risk losing his heir over one girl."

"You bet my fucking life on Matteo's mercy?" I snap, voice shaking with disbelief and rage. "You put your daughter's survival on the table like a fucking poker chip and prayed some other man would step in and do the job you were too much of a coward to fucking do yourself?" My voice rises, but it doesn't waver. It burns. "You didn't protect me. You outsourced me."

He lowers his head, shoulders slumping like the weight of the truth finally crushed what little spine he had left.

But it's too fucking late.

Shame doesn't undo what he did. And regret doesn't bring back the pieces he let them take.

Behind him, Matteo's grip tightens on the gun, jaw clenched so hard I swear I hear it grind.

His voice comes low, lethal, soaked in venom and fury. "You were supposed to fucking die before you let anything happen to her," he snarls. "That's what it means to be a father. You don't sell your own fucking blood to save your sorry ass."

My father flinches. His eyes flick to me wary now. Afraid. Because he knows that Matteo would end him right here, right now, and sleep like a fucking baby after.

"Emery," he says.

"No." Matteo's voice cuts through the room, sharp enough to draw blood. "You don't get to say her name. Not now. Not ever. You lost that fucking right the second you handed her over—tossed her away, treating her as if she meant nothing. As if she was beneath you."

His eyes burn through him, a slow, lethal fire.

"She's mine now. Mine to protect. Mine to fight for. And believe me..." His lips part, the words spilling out in a vow carved into flesh. "She'll never be collateral damage again. Not while I'm still fucking breathing."

And as I stare down at my father, the man who chose survival over blood, I realize something.

He's already dead to me.

Now it's just a matter of deciding if he deserves to keep breathing or not.

Chapter Eighteen

Matteo

I hold the gun steady against the bastard's head, finger hovering over the trigger, pressure coiled so tight in my chest it's a miracle I haven't snapped. My pulse is so loud it drowns out everything but her.

I want him fucking dead. I want him gone for what he did to her.

But this isn't my call. It's hers.

Emery stands in front of us, back straight, eyes burning like the fire that forged her into something unstoppable.

Fuck, she's beautiful like this. Untouchable and unshaken. Rage and hurt carved into every breath, every inch of her defiance.

She hasn't flinched once. Not when he begged, not when he lied. Not even when he looked her in the eye and tried to rewrite the past as if she didn't remember every fucking second burned into her bones.

I can't stop watching her. Can't stop feeling it. This need to protect her, to fucking worship her for surviving what he tried to bury.

He's still breathing, but only because she hasn't told me otherwise. And if she does... If she gives me the word, I'll pull the trigger without blinking. I'll end Dante Moretti right here, right now, no fucking regrets. Because Emery's mine now, and no one ever hurts what's mine and walks away from it.

She takes one step forward. There's no fear in her eyes, just fire. She's focused, fucking lethal.

She holds out her hand. Palm up, fingers steady. Eyes locked on mine, unblinking, unwavering, like she already knows I'll give her what she's asking for. What she's fucking earned.

I freeze, for just a breath. Because fuck... A part of me believed she'd let me bear the burden. That she'd let me be the one to end him—to become the executioner she shouldn't have to be.

I wanted to be the one to erase him from her life, to pull the trigger and wipe away his stain.

To spare her the sound, the recoil, the weight of watching his body hit the floor.

But I see it, clear as day in the way her eyes burn. In the hard line of her jaw. In the way her breath barely falters, like she's holding the weight of the world inside her chest.

This isn't about revenge. It's not about blood. It's about reclaiming what was stolen from her—her voice, her power, her goddamn sense of self.

This isn't my moment to take. It never was.

So I let go of the need to shield her from this, of the part of me that aches to pull the trigger. Instead, I give her what she came for. What she fought and bled for.

Because this choice, this justice, this reckoning—it's hers. Every last piece of it.

My hand moves toward her, the weight of the gun heavy in my palm.

Her fingers graze mine, trembling slightly—barely holding herself together, as if one more touch might shatter her.

Then she takes it. Firm. Certain.

As though she's held it a thousand times in her mind. As if the steel always belonged to her, never to me.

Her hand wraps around the grip like it's part of her now, an extension of her rage, her grief, her goddamn will to survive.

And in that second, I know. She's taking the power back.

She raises the gun and aims at the man who sold her out.

The muzzle meets his forehead... clean, centered, absolute.

Her finger wraps around the trigger. No twitch. No hesitation.

Just silence, thick, crushing, like it could smother us both.

I can't breathe. My chest locked tight, the air too thick to pull in.

But I don't move. I don't blink.

I just watch her, the girl I love, the woman who could bring this entire fucking empire to its knees, standing there, steady. Unshaken.

She's fucking beautiful in this moment. The way she's holding that gun with such calm, the power in her stillness, her rage simmering just beneath the surface.

And if she pulls that trigger... If she ends this here? I won't feel an ounce of remorse.

I'll watch him fall like the fucking piece of shit he is, and I won't feel a damn thing—except the satisfaction of her finally taking back what's hers. I'll hold her in the aftermath, right there on the blood-stained floor. I'll fuck her in his blood, and show her how much I love her. Show her how goddamn beautiful it is when she owns everything—her pain, her power, her future.

But she pauses. And fuck, the quiet suddenly feels louder. Her eyes stay locked on him, her breath shallow but steady.

I hold my breath too, watching her. Waiting. This is her moment, and whatever she chooses, I'll stand beside her.

Seconds crawl by, each one heavy, like the whole world is pressing down on us.

Then finally, slowly, her hand begins to lower.

The gun drifts down with it, her grip still tight, knuckles white, but it's no longer aimed at him.

She steps back, each movement controlled like she's shedding the last remnants of his hold on her.

The gun drops to her side as she stares him down, disgust etched into every line of her face, contempt curling at her lips—a warning in the shape of a snarl.

"Fuck you," she says. Every word is a strike, tearing the last vestiges of his control straight from her soul. "I won't become you. I won't turn into a monster just because you didn't have the spine to be a fucking father."

And damn, my chest aches with pride. I've never been more in awe of her. Of how beautifully she just ripped herself free from the poison he's spent a lifetime trying to pour into her veins.

She's not just Emery in this moment. She's fury wrapped in skin. A fucking storm with a pulse. Every breath she drags in is defiance. Every word she throws lands like fire-tipped bullets. And fuck, I see it now... the strength that crawled through the wreckage, the fire that didn't just survive the chaos. She became the fucking chaos. And she's still burning.

She doesn't bend. Doesn't flinch. She rises. Again and again. Like a goddamn rebellion, carved into her skin and bone.

She's everything I'm not. Everything I was never allowed to be. And everything I fucking still crave.

I'm the lucky bastard who gets to stand beside her. The one who gets to worship her—my hands, my mouth, my cock, my body all devoted to her. Who gets to hear her fall apart when I fuck her like she's sacred. Because she is.

She turns, her gaze locking with mine, eyes blazing with rage, pain, and power.

Without a word, she hands me back the gun. It's not just a gesture. It's a declaration. She didn't need to pull the trigger to take control. She already has it.

I grab the bastard by the collar, yanking him up so hard the chair screeches across the floor. He chokes as I shove him toward the door, my grip punishing, unforgiving. Every muscle in my body's still wired tight, adrenaline flooding through me, synced to the fury burning inside her.

I glance back, needing to see her.

Emery hasn't moved. She stands right where she was, feet planted, shoulders squared. Eyes burning bright, like she just stepped out of hell and owned it.

She's not the girl I used to know. She's something more.

And fuck, I've never wanted her more than I do in this moment.

It takes everything in me not to stop, not to turn around, grab her by the back of the neck, and kiss her so hard it leaves a mark. Because right now, all I want is her. Her mouth crushed against mine, her body locked to me, her thighs hooked around my waist while my cock slides in deep and pulls a moan from her throat, my name the only goddamn thing she can remember.

But we're not there yet.

We have to finish this first. She deserves a clean ending, real closure, before either of us can finally breathe again. Before I get to rip away every last layer between us and have her the way I've been dying to for years.

I keep moving, shoving the bastard toward the truck, each step weighed down by the rage still burning in my chest.

Dante stumbles, weak, pathetic.

I yank him upright by the collar, my voice dropping low, vibrating with everything I'm holding back.

"You fall again, and I'll drag your sorry ass the rest of the way. Face first."

He doesn't speak, doesn't even glance in my direction. Maybe he finally understands now. This ends my way. No more fucking deals, and no more running.

Behind me, I hear Emery. Her footsteps echo in the quiet. There's no hesitation in her stride.

When I reach the truck, I shove the bastard into the back seat without a second thought for how he lands. He grunts, his wrists twisting as I yank them behind his back, cinching the zip ties tight enough to remind him who the fuck's in control now.

I slam the door so hard the whole frame rattles.

And then I turn.

Emery walks toward me, the wind tearing through her hair, strands whipping across her face—pure storm and salvation wrapped in one. Sunlight ignites in her eyes. Wild. Fearless. Fucking glorious. A vision made to be worshipped.

And I feel it clawing at me. The need to take her, drag her into me, bury my hands in her hair with my mouth on her skin.

I move toward her, until I'm close enough that only she can hear. Close enough to breathe her in, to feel the heat radiating off her skin.

"You're fucking incredible," I murmur, voice rough, low, soaked in everything I've been holding back. "Standing there, facing him down like that... you weren't just strong, Em. You were a fucking queen."

She meets my gaze, and for a moment, something soft flickers behind all that fire in her eyes.

"I wasn't going to give him the satisfaction," she whispers, voice tight with emotion. "He's already taken enough from me."

"He'll never take another fucking thing," I say, my fingers brushing along her jaw, tilting her face toward mine. My touch is gentle, but everything inside me is anything but. "Not from you. Not while I'm still breathing." My thumb traces the edge of her cheek, possessive, steady. "You ready to do this?" I ask.

She nods, the smallest smile pulling at her lips.

I curl my fingers around hers, lead her around the front of the truck and open the passenger side door. She slides into the front seat without a word.

I round the hood, drop into the driver's seat, and twist the key. The engine growls to life.

In the rearview, I catch sight of the bastard slumped in the back. Cowering. Shaking. A fucking ghost of a man.

I look him dead in the eye, voice low and lethal. "You better pray my father is in a merciful mood today," I say, the words sharp. "Because if it were up to me?" I pause, letting the silence stretch. "You'd already be rotting in a shallow fucking grave, wrapped in all the lies you bled to keep breathing."

Then I look at Emery. Head held high, spine straight. She stares down the whole fucking world, daring it to blink first. There's no fear in her. Whatever's waiting at the end of this ride... it should be scared of her.

And right then, I fucking feel it in my bones. Whatever my father has planned, whatever sick fucking game he's playing, he'll learn that the boy he raised isn't the same man driving toward him now. He's going to want blood for this. And he can have it. But it won't be hers. It'll be mine.

The road hums in silence. Except for him. Her father, the coward in the backseat choking on his own goddamn lies.

He hasn't spoken since we dragged him out—trash, nothing more. Not a single fucking word. He just sits there, small, sweating through his sins. Every breath he takes sounds like a fucking confession. It's sharp and shallow, as if his lungs are too scared to fill all the way, as though even they know he doesn't deserve the air.

I hear that soft, pathetic panting. Like fear is crawling up his throat and strangling him from the inside out.

Good.

Let the fucker suffer. Let it settle in his chest and crack every rib. Let it twist around his spine and remind him with every mile that this is borrowed time.

He shifts once, barely, and the leather creaks underneath him. I don't even look back. Just tighten my grip on the wheel and say nothing, because the longer the silence drags, the louder it gets. And I fucking want him to sit in that noise. I want him to stew in every second of it, in every fucking mile that takes us closer to the man who turned me into what I am.

He's scared. Not just of what's waiting at the end of this road, but of me. Which he should be because if my father doesn't end him, I fucking will.

I glance at Emery. She doesn't speak, just stares ahead like she's carved from stone and lit from the inside with something untouchable. Chin up, shoulders squared, eyes locked on the road. She doesn't even acknowledge the sorry fuck curled up in the backseat, wheezing through his fear. She doesn't need to, because she's already won.

We're driving straight toward the monster most people would sell their soul to escape. And she's walking into it as if it's just another fight she intends to finish. As though she's already counted the cost and decided that pain and fate are part of the price. And fuck me, I've seen men lead armies with less fire in their eyes. I've watched killers, warlords, empire-builders stare down death and grin. But none of them had this.

That quiet, relentless strength. This brutal grace that doesn't ask for power it just fucking commands it. She took her crown without ceremony, without mercy. And I swear to God, I'd follow her into any war she wanted.

My phone buzzes. I already know who it is before I look. The weight in my gut tells me. The kind of dread you don't shake. The kind you're born with when you carry his blood.

King Prick: Time's up, Matteo.

That's all it says. Three words. Cold and final. Loaded like a fucking gun.

I slam the brakes, gravel spraying like shrapnel as the truck jerks off the road and skids to a stop beneath a canopy of thick, overgrown trees. The engine growls once before settling into a low, threatening purr.

My father wasn't supposed to move first. We were supposed to walk in strong on our own terms. But now...

Now we're walking into his game. His rules. His arena.

He's moved the board. Flipped the fucking table, and now we're not the hunters anymore, we're the fucking prey.

I drag a hand over my face, rage building under my skin like pressure behind a dam.

"Matteo?" Emery's voice is cautious, laced with worry.

I hold up a finger, needing just one second. Just a breath. One move that won't get her killed. Because that's what this is now... a fucking countdown to the moment my father sees her and puts a bullet in her skull just to prove a point.

To teach me another one of his twisted fucked up lessons. About loyalty. About weakness. About what happens when you love something enough to bleed for it.

I quickly type, adrenaline spiking through every nerve.

Matteo: I've got something you want more than my head.

The pause drags… seconds stretch into eternity, my heart a live grenade in my chest.

Then the screen lights up.

King Prick: You're in no position to negotiate, son.

I clench my jaw, thumbs flying again, fighting the urge to put my fist through the dash.

Matteo: I have the traitor. Alive. But I'm not walking blindly into your guns. We meet somewhere neutral. No guards. No bullshit. Just you, me, and your little fucking traitor.

Silence again. Longer this time. He's making me sweat. Deciding whether he wants to crush me now or make me bleed first.

I can practically feel his rage seeping through the screen… slow and poisonous, the kind that comes wrapped in a smile and ends in someone's body hitting the floor.

Emery watches me. Intense. Quiet.

Her father shifts in the back seat, nerves turning his spine to jelly. He opens his mouth, then shuts it. Smart fucking choice.

Then… finally, my phone buzzes again.

King Prick: Name your place.

My grip tightens around the phone like I could crush the bastard through the glass.

He took the bait. A cold smile pulls at my mouth, it's twisted, full of the kind of satisfaction that comes with getting one up on the fucker.

I type fast, fingers steady despite the storm rising in my chest.

Matteo: The old slaughterhouse. One hour.

I toss the phone onto the dash, the burn of it still crawling up my palm.

I turn toward Emery. "We have a meeting," I say, voice low, flat. "Neutral ground."

"You trust him to keep it neutral?"

"Fuck no," I breathe. "He'll bring his whole fucking army. He needs the show. The performance. He needs to remind me, and every fucker watching, that he's still the one pulling the strings. This is how he does it. Smoke and blood and power plays."

She nods once, then flicks her gaze to the back seat, where her father shrinks further into himself, barely breathing.

"You sure you want to do it like this, Matteo?" she asks. "We can do it another way if you want, I have something—"

I lean in, cutting her off before she can finish that sentence. "We have leverage now. We set the terms. We control this." My fingers brush her jaw, gentle, aching, as if it might be the last time I get to touch her. "I promised I'd protect you," I say, softer now. "And I fucking meant it, Em. Things have changed. I won't have you there. I can't."

She jerks back, eyes blazing. "No, Matteo," she snaps. "You don't get to shut me out. Not now. Not after everything." Her hands ball into fists in her lap, voice shaking—not with fear, but fury. "I won't let you walk in there by yourself like you're some goddamn martyr. You're not doing this alone. Let me help. You don't get to decide that for me. I have—"

I give her a look that should say it all. Should shut it down before it starts. Then I lift my hand, cup the side of her face, soft, but final. "No. You are not going anywhere near him. He will fucking kill you just to prove a point. Just to remind me who holds the leash."

She opens her mouth, but I don't let her speak. Not this time.

My voice cuts like steel. "This isn't up for fucking debate."

This conversation is over. There's no fucking way I'm letting her anywhere near that prick.

I throw the car into gear and pull out hard, my pulse pounding in my ears.

I drive hard and fast. Every turn burned into muscle memory. I don't speak; I don't even look her way. I keep my shoulders rigid, my grip locked tight on the wheel.

I know exactly where I'll leave her. Somewhere no one will ever think to check.

A run-down house, half-swallowed by the woods, rotting into the earth like everything else that's been forgotten. Two miles up the road from the slaughterhouse. It's quiet. Hidden. Just far enough to keep her out of his sight, just close enough for her to find her way, if for some fucking reason I don't make it out.

CHAPTER NINETEEN

MATTEO

I park behind the rusted carcass of an old semi, its cab gutted, metal torn open like something died screaming inside it. It's cloaked in shadow, tucked far enough back to keep me hidden, but close enough to watch everything.

I kill the engine. The silence that follows is thick, pressing in like it knows something I don't.

Glancing at my phone, I see the message still glowing on the screen, still pulsing—a fucking warning set to detonate:

Time's up, Matteo.

Those words are carved into me now, branded into my skin, a promise I'll bleed for if I have to.

I scan the lot.

No cars, no movement, no guards. No sign of him. Just open space and the eerie stillness of a place built for violence.

But that's how my father works. He doesn't show his hand, he lets you sweat, lets you start to question whether the bullet's coming from in front of you or behind. He's already set the stage, and I'm already playing my part.

I push the truck door open and step out into the glare—daylight crashing down like a goddamn spotlight. There's nowhere to hide. No shadows, no cover. Just the wide, empty sprawl of the slaughterhouse lot... rusted bones, crumbling wreckage, and a silence so heavy it's thick enough to choke on.

I yank open the back door and haul Emery's father out by the collar, dragging his sorry ass the way you'd rip out garbage on collection day. He stumbles hard, feet skidding on gravel, hands twitching with a pathetic attempt to mask the fear, he's failing, and we both know it.

Good.

He should be afraid of what's waiting for him. Of my father. Of the fucking consequences finally sinking their teeth in after all this time. Because I'm not the same man who shoved him into that truck. I'm colder now. Crueler. There's nothing left to lose, not with her still out there, waiting for me to come back.

Emery fought me. Christ, she screamed. That fury in her voice... it told me everything. The second I walked away, something inside her shattered. Going into this alone wasn't just dangerous or reckless—it cut deeper. It was a fucking betrayal. And beneath all that rage, the hurt was carved into her face, plain as day.

She yelled. Shoved me. Spat every filthy name she could think of, as if the venom might keep her from splintering. Hurt laced with heat, heartbreak dressed in battle gear. And yeah, she looked at me with murder in her eyes, but it wasn't hate. It was love, bleeding out through the cracks. Desperate. Messy. The kind that claws at your chest and screams don't you fucking die, because if you do, I won't survive it.

But in the end... she let me go. She trusted me.

I watched her fall silent. Watched her eyes fill with all the things she wouldn't say.

I left her in that crumbling house, surrounded by ghosts and silence, with nothing but my promise to come back. It was the only way I could protect her.

It felt like tearing my heart out of my chest and handing it to her still beating. But I have to do this for us.

My grip tightens as I drag her father forward. He whimpers something. Some pitiful excuse, maybe a plea, but I don't hear it. I don't want to. I've heard enough lies to last a lifetime.

The slaughterhouse doors groan open, long and low—a warning dragging through the air. Every step we take inside echoes, loud and hollow. The cracked concrete beneath our boots is stained with old blood and bad memories, soaked in so deep the walls still scream with it.

And then, he steps out from the far end of the room, sliding from the shadows like the devil himself.

My father. Alone. Hands empty. But I know better.

His men are here, watching, waiting. Hidden in the walls with fingers wrapped around triggers and orders whispered in their ears like gospel.

He stops a few feet away, posture easy, almost relaxed, as if he's not standing in the middle of a graveyard built from the deaths of those who wronged him.

Then he speaks. His voice colder than the steel he once taught me to kill with.

"I did warn you what betrayal would cost, Matteo," he says, eyes locked on mine. "And you still chose a fucking woman over your own blood?"

He says the word woman with the weight of filth in his tone. To him, Emery isn't a person—she's a passing whim, a distraction. He sees her as weakness, a soft spot carved for the blade.

But he's got it fucking wrong. Loving her didn't make me weak. It made me fucking dangerous.

My muscles strain beneath the skin, like everything inside me is coiled too tight to breathe.

"I chose my own path," I say, voice sharp, carved from everything he made me into. "You taught me to take what's mine, to protect what matters. And that's exactly what I'm fucking doing."

He laughs. It's bitter, hollow, a sound that scrapes against the inside of my skull like nails on steel. There's no humor in it. Just venom.

"What matters in this life is loyalty," he snaps. "Family. And you spat in my face the second you killed Rocco for that bitch."

I grab Dante and shove him forward, watching him stumble, a coward through and through. He drops to his knees, hands scraping against the concrete, breath hitching, aware that one wrong move means his end.

"This piece of shit is yours," I growl. "He betrayed you. Gave her up to save his own skin. So go ahead. Take your revenge. Paint the fucking floor with him if that's what it takes to remind yourself you're still a man."

I step back, heart pounding, rage bubbling beneath the surface, a fuse seconds from detonation.

"But after this?" I lock eyes with him, unflinching, standing my ground. "I'm done."

My father's eyes narrow, his posture stiffening, that quiet fury starting to bleed through his polished control.

"You think handing over one traitor absolves you of your sins?" he snarls, stepping forward. "You're my blood, Matteo. You don't get to walk away. You answer to me."

I don't move. Don't blink.

I let his fury hit me like a wave and I fucking stand in it.

"No," I say. "I don't answer to anyone anymore. Not you, and not your fucking empire." I take a step closer, and for the first time in my life, he shifts back.

"This is my last gift to you," I say, nodding to Emery's father, still choking on fear at our feet. "A traitor on a silver fucking platter. Do whatever the hell you want with him. Shoot him, string him up, carve your pride back out of his skin. I don't give a shit." I take another step, closing the distance between us until we're toe to toe. "After this, I'm gone. You let me go. You let her go. And you keep your dogs on their fucking leashes."

His nostrils flare, face tight with rage. "You think you can threaten me? You think you walk out of this and there's not a bullet waiting for you somewhere down the line? You're still mine, Matteo. You always will fucking be mine. You walk, I drag you back in chains."

"You come after us again, and I'll burn down every piece of your precious kingdom." I shove him back, my hand still trembling. "I'll bury your legacy so deep not even your ghosts will remember you."

"I always knew you were ruthless, Matteo," he sneers. "But choosing her? That makes you weak."

"No," I say. "Choosing her makes me stronger than you ever fucking were."

The muscle in his jaw jerks, barely tethered to restraint. That same old power-hungry darkness slides across his face, a shadow sweeping over a grave. His mouth curls, bitter and cruel, chewing on the taste of lost control.

And for a second...just one...the world holds still.

Then I hear it.

The soft, unmistakable shuffle of boots across concrete.

The dry click of safeties coming off.

The sound of war winding up.

I don't even fucking flinch. Because I know that sound. I was raised on it. It's the music that played behind every lesson he carved into me. Pain, loyalty, obedience. I know the rhythm of it better than my own goddamn heartbeat.

From the shadows, they step out. Four... no, five. Guns raised, barrels gleaming beneath the cracked skylight, shining with promises meant to end in blood. My father's soldiers. His dogs. The same ones who used to train me. Now aiming down their sights, eyes cold with loyalty sharpened into a weapon, treating me as just another target on their kill list.

They spread out, tactical, perfect, cutting off every path, every exit. Except the one that goes straight through them.

And fuck it... if that's what it takes... then that's the path I'll take.

I don't move or reach for my weapon. I don't give them the satisfaction.

I just smile, the kind that cuts without ever needing a blade.

My father watches me, his face carved from stone, eyes dead behind the ice. That same cold detached look he's worn his whole life. Emotion was a disease he cured himself of a long time ago.

"You thought I'd let you walk out of here?" he says, voice almost amused, mocking, like this is a game and I've already fucking lost. "You're not my son anymore. You're a fucking liability." His mouth curls into a cruel, wicked smile, razor-thin and soaked in satisfaction. "And liabilities... they get erased."

He pulls a weapon from inside his jacket... smooth, practiced, like he's been waiting for this moment since the second I dropped Rocco.

The gun comes up fast, barrel leveled at my chest.

I don't move. Not a fucking inch. Because I know how this works. One wrong twitch, one breath too deep, and his dogs will paint the walls with me. Turn me into a fucking bonfire, then sleep soundly afterward, not a flicker of guilt in sight.

My eyes stay locked on his. Ice meeting ice.

"Then pull the fucking trigger yourself," I shout. "Or are you too much of a coward to finish what you started?"

His nostrils flare, breath shallow and pissed. Eyes narrowed, he steps closer, so close I can smell the gun oil and cologne clinging to his skin. The weight of everything we've never said settles between us like smoke.

"You think you're ready to die for her?" he hisses, voice sharp enough to bleed.

I don't blink.

"No," I rasp, my voice thick with everything he never taught me. Loyalty, love. The kind of love that doesn't kneel. Doesn't run. "I'm ready to kill for her."

The men around me shift, subtle but telling, hands tightening on their rifles, muscles coiled, waiting for the command. One nod. One twitch from him. That's all it would take to end me.

And still... he doesn't give it.

Because I fucking know. The second his mask slips, that tiny pause, that flicker of hesitation, it's there. A crack in the armor. Barely visible, but I know my father too well not to see it.

And the way he's looking at me, like I'm the ghost of a future he never planned for. One he can't shape or bend. Can't fucking control anymore. Because I'm not just his son. I'm his heir. I'm the thing he molded with blood and fire and all the sharp edges he carved into me.

Killing me doesn't just sever bloodlines. It cuts the throat of his legacy.

And he knows it. Plus if he kills me here, in front of his men, in the place where he turned boys into monsters his men will ask themselves a question he can't afford: If he can kill his own son, what the fuck does loyalty mean?

And that's the one thing he can't survive. Doubt. But no bullets come. Just silence. Then he nods.

A single, quiet motion. Small. Precise. That's all it takes.

His soldiers move like shadows. Trained, merciless, silent as death. They're on me before I can shift, grabbing my arms and wrenching them back with a force that sends white-hot pain ripping through my shoulders. I grunt, but I don't scream. I won't give him that.

They shove me down, my knees hitting the floor first, then my face slamming into the concrete. Hard. Grit tears into my cheek, and blood bursts in my mouth. It's bitter, flooding my tongue like punishment.

This is what he wanted. Not to kill me. Not to break me. To remind me who the fuck I belong to.

"Stay fucking put," one of them snarls, pressing his boot between my shoulder blades the way a hunter pins down prey, just flesh, just a trophy, nothing more.

The pressure grinds into bone, pinning me like an animal, and it takes everything I have not to move, not to snap, not to rip his fucking leg out from under him and crack his skull open on the concrete.

I wait. Breathing heavy, jaw clenched so tight my molars threaten to crack from the pressure. Blood pools in my mouth, all rust and rage.

My father steps past me. Calm. Unhurried—this is just business to him. As though I'm not even worth a glance.

His polished shoes, perfect, expensive, soulless, stop inches from my face, the leather catching the fractured light above like it's something holy.

I tilt my head, just enough to see him standing over Dante Moretti.

The man's still on his knees, trembling like a coward. And he looks smaller by the second, shrinking under the weight of the reckoning he helped build but never had the spine to own.

And for a heartbeat, I forget the pain in my body, because I know what's coming.

"You," my father spits, disgust curling each syllable as if he's choking on bile. "I gave you everything. Power. Respect. My fucking trust. And you repay me by slithering into the shadows—a rat crawling through the same dirt you once sent others to die in?"

Emery's father shudders. He's weak and pathetic. Sweat clings to his face, his skin ashen, as though he's already partway to the grave.

"Please," he breathes, barely audible. A whimper, not a defense. "I didn't... I was—"

"You were what?" my father growls, stepping in so close the bastard goes stiff, spine pulled tight as if fear alone might snap it in half. "I made you. Protected you. Gave you a seat at my table when you were nothing but bloodstained hands and empty threats. And still you have the fucking nerve to betray me." He circles him, slow and deliberate, a predator savoring the moment before the kill. "Now look at you... shaking, pathetic, trembling the way a mutt does after pissing on the wrong boot. Begging."

Dante flinches like he's been struck, the shame and fear rolling off him in waves.

My father crouches beside him, calm now. Too fucking calm. That's when he's at his most dangerous. His voice drops to a low, slicing whisper.

"Tell me," he leans in close, their faces inches apart, breath hot with fury, "was it worth it?"

"N-no," Dante stammers like a fucking coward, voice cracking, as his body shudders uncontrollably. "It was a mistake, please... I didn't mean—"

"You're goddamn right it was a mistake." My father straightens, rising with all the weight of a man who knows he owns every soul in this place. All except mine. His expression is stone. But his eyes... fuck, his eyes burn like fire eating through flesh. "And now you're going to fucking pay for it. Slowly. Painfully. Second by fucking second."

From where I'm pinned, cheek pressed against the rough concrete, I watch as Emery's father crumbles. The tremble in his limbs turns violent, his breathing spiraling into ragged panic.

And then it happens.

The bastard pisses himself.

The sharp, acrid scent hits the air, cutting through the metallic tang of blood and dust. The last shred of pride leaking out of him, soaking the floor beneath his knees.

My father stares down at him, lips curled in disgust. He shakes his head slowly, like he's looking at roadkill that used to mean something.

"Pathetic," he mutters, not even looking at him anymore, as if the sight alone offends him. Then he turns to face me and gives a single nod.

The men don't hesitate.

They haul me to my feet. Their hands clamping down on my arms so tight I swear I can feel bone scrape against bone. Pain rips through my shoulders, a deep, dragging throb, but I bite it down. I don't give them the satisfaction. I keep my eyes locked on my father.

Cold.

Unflinching.

Exactly how he trained me.

But not for the reasons he ever fucking understood.

The stench of piss still clings to the air, thick and sour. Leaking from the broken shell of Emery's father, who's collapsed in a quivering heap at his feet. The man who once held power in his fists now trembles like a kicked dog, too far gone to even lift his head.

My father stares down at him, disgust carved deep into every cruel line of his face. He doesn't rush. Doesn't speak. Just stands there, letting the man at his feet feel every second of it.

Then, slowly, he lifts the gun. No warning. Just the cold certainty of a man who's done this too many times to pretend it means something anymore.

"You're a waste of fucking breath," he says, almost bored. As if the man groveling at his feet is just another name to strike off the books.

He shifts the barrel, tilting it slightly, and presses it to the side of the traitor's head.

Not centered. Not clean. Cruel.

Dante jerks, flinching like he still thinks there's room for mercy. His eyes go wide. Pure panic, glistening with tears. His breath hitches, shaky and broken, chest rising in shallow bursts as the finality of it sinks in.

"Please—" he chokes, the word collapsing out of him as though it might save his life.

My father doesn't flinch. No hesitation, no second thoughts. He just pulls the trigger.

The gunshot tears through the silence, a brutal, deafening crack that ricochets off the walls and punches straight through the moment. A scream made of smoke and steel, ripping the air apart.

Blood sprays across the concrete... hot, violent, final. It splatters his shoes. Paints the floor.

Dante drops instantly, his body collapsing with a dull thud, eyes wide open but already empty.

My father exhales through his nose, calm as ever, like he just took out the trash.

"You see that, Matteo?"

His voice rings out, calm and cruel as he turns toward me slowly. The gun is still in his hand, smoke curling lazily from the barrel as if it's the ghost of a prayer no one ever bothered to answer.

"This is what weakness gets you," he says, gesturing to the lifeless heap bleeding out on the concrete. "A bullet. On your knees. Covered in your own fucking shame."

The words slip from my mouth before I can stop them, laced with every ounce of hate I've swallowed for years. "Better fucking dead than crawling at your feet."

His smile vanishes. Just snaps off his face like a switch.

In one swift, lethal move, he closes the distance—faster than I can brace. He grabs me by the collar, yanking me forward like I'm still some kid he can drag into line. Then he slams the gun into my head, hard, a crack of bone against steel that rattles straight through my skull.

His men tighten their grip, clamping down on my arms and pushing my knees back onto the floor. Their fists dig into my biceps, crushing down with all the force of men who think pain is the language I'll finally understand.

They think they can hold me. Break me. Force me to beg. They have no fucking idea.

I stay still. Spine straight. Shoulders squared.

He steps into me and lifts the gun, the barrel aimed squarely at my head. It's meant to intimidate, to remind me who still holds the power in this place. It's a performance. The same tired threat he's used a thousand times to keep men crawling at his feet.

But I don't flinch. Instead, I move.

I lean into it, pushing the barrel until the cold steel is pressed flush against my skin. I drive it harder into my own forehead. The metal digs deep, bruising already, unforgiving in the way it kisses bone.

I don't break eye contact. I want him to see it. This isn't fear. It's a challenge. I'm daring him, right here, right now. Because if he wants to kill me, he's going to have to do it while looking into the eyes of the man he created and the man he will never fucking control again.

My heart pounds. A brutal, violent rhythm slamming against my ribs like it's trying to break free, but I force myself to breathe slowly, steady, controlled. I won't give him the satisfaction. I won't let him see fear on my face. Not now. Not ever.

"You were supposed to inherit everything," he growls. "I built an empire for you. For our family." He spits the word like it still means something. "And you threw it all away for a fucking girl."

I meet his eyes, unflinching. Let him rage. Let him scream. Let him writhe in his own delusion. He can't reach what I feel. He can't shatter what's already been reforged. He doesn't get to erase what's mine.

His snarl sharpens, lips curling in frustration as the silence stretches.

"Say something," he snaps, voice cracking just slightly around the edges as he shoves the gun harder against my skull. "Don't think I won't do it because I fucking will"

But I don't break. I never fucking will.

Even with the barrel pressed to my head, even with his men holding me down like I'm nothing but a body to be disposed of, I hold steady. Because in this moment, if these are my last minutes on this fucked-up earth, it isn't his face I see. It's not the stone-cold bastards holding me down.

It's her.

Emery.

Her eyes burning fierce, defiant, beautiful like a fucking wildfire that won't be tamed. Her mouth curling into that stubborn, reckless smile I fell in love with before I even knew what love was. That's what fills my vision. That's what grounds me when the world is shaking.

If I die here, on this blood-streaked floor, I won't regret it. Because I chose her. And I'd choose her again. Every. Single. Fucking. Time.

Chapter Twenty

EMERY

I never promised Matteo I'd stay away. He told me to. Demanded it. Like leaving me behind was some noble fucking sacrifice.

As if shutting me out of the war would somehow keep me safe. But I'd already spent half my life dancing on the edge of a blade.

But what Matteo didn't know… well actually what none of them knew, was that I already had a card to play. One my father left behind.

Long before Matteo ever showed up at that diner, full of fury and hands that made my body betray every ounce of common sense, I was already surviving. Already moving. Before the ropes. Before the threats. Before his cock slipped between my thighs and turned my world sideways, I had already learned how to run. How to disappear. How to hide in plain fucking sight.

When I bolted from my old life, I didn't grab much. A box, some cash, and whatever scraps of me that hadn't been shattered yet. And at the bottom of that box there was a flash drive. Small. Black. Unmarked.

My father's carelessness turned out to be my salvation.

I didn't open it right away. Didn't even breathe near it. I kept it buried, tucked between old clothes because something about it made my skin itch.

But I waited. Because opening it meant facing whatever the fuck was inside, and I wasn't ready. Not then.

At first, I didn't know what kind of poison lived on that drive. Didn't dare to look. Just shoved it to the bottom of my bag, pretending it wasn't burning through the fabric, pretending it wasn't ticking with every breath. But months later, alone in some shitty motel, living off vending machine dinners and silence, I finally cracked it open.

And fuck me... The files weren't just incriminating. They were lethal.

Bank accounts soaked in blood money. Bribes stacked like bodies. Kill orders signed off with no hesitation.

It was all there.

Enough to collapse the whole kingdom Alessandro De Luca built in blood and bullets. Enough to put a target on my back that would never fucking fade.

I didn't just find secrets. It was power. Enough to bring down an empire.

And when the time came, I'd be ready to make it bleed. I had my match—my goddamn firestarter.

One strike, and I'd burn it all to the ground.

I transferred every file to a secure drive, buried it behind walls of encryption so thick even the devil himself would struggle to claw through. I told myself I was just being careful. That I'd never need it.

But I've learned hope is a fragile lie. So I prepared. Just in case.

When Matteo dropped me off and told me to stay hidden, he shoved a burner phone into my hand. Said if he didn't return in six hours, it meant his father had killed him. That I was to run. That he loved me with every broken, bloodstained piece of himself.

But you know what… I'm done fucking running. I'm not leaving him to face the wolves alone. Not when I know how sharp my teeth are.

The moment that burner hit my palm, I knew I could crack what I needed, pull the access, unlock the file. My bullet, locked, loaded, and aimed. This time, I shoot first.

By the time I reach the slaughterhouse, my legs are trembling, lungs clawing for air like they're trying to tear out of my chest. Sweat slicks my back, my shirt glued to me—damp, choking, suffocating.

I ran the whole way. Didn't think. Didn't stop. Just kept moving. Like if I slowed down for even a second, the weight of it all would crush me into the ground.

The late afternoon sun hits the rusted roof in hard streaks. Dust hangs thick in the air, curling in the light like ghosts too tired to haunt anymore. My boots crunch over gravel as I press against the warped metal siding, every nerve in my body stretched tight and screaming.

Inside, voices echo. Low and rough, the kind of sound that promises pain. The kind that means blood will follow. I can't make out the words yet, but I don't need to. My gut already knows, plus I didn't come here to listen.

I slip in closer. Quiet and precise. I'm not Emery right now. I'm every sharp edge my father forged without realizing it. Every sleepless night. Every wound I stitched shut with my own hands. I'm the result of his betrayal. The weapon he never saw coming. And make no mistake—I didn't come here to fucking beg.

I move toward the open doorway. The air slams into me, a fist to the gut. Blood, sweat, rot. It hangs heavy, soaked into the walls, steeped in memory. My lungs twitch, ready to choke, but I don't let them. I won't give them the fucking satisfaction.

Then I see him. Matteo. On his knees. The king's son, brought low, a fucking traitor to the throne. And towering over him stands his father, Alessandro. The monster in the crown. A goddamn executioner in silk. He presses the gun to Matteo's forehead, not hesitating, not blinking. A baptism in lead, blood, and betrayal.

Matteo's face is bloodied, streaked with defiance. He's not broken. Not begging. It's that kind of fuck-you fire that dares you to pull the trigger. Watching him kneel like that… shoulders squared, jaw set, eyes burning with wildfire rage, it splinters something deep in my chest.

I grip the doorframe, the pressure in my hands the only thing anchoring me upright, fingers digging into the splintered wood. Every muscle in me coils, pressure building in my chest, ready to detonate. To run in there. Scream. Tear the fucking world apart. But I don't. I force it down, bury it deep. Because this isn't the moment for feeling. It's the moment for control.

I draw the burner from my pocket, hands shaking like they already know I'm stepping into a blood-soaked final act. One tap. That's all it takes. One fucking tap, and the empire crumbles.

I suck in a breath, hold the burner screen out in front of me, and brace. The second I cross into the slaughterhouse; it's like the world splits down the middle.

Every gun in the room snaps toward me, metal mouths hungry to shred through flesh and bone. Shouts explode. Orders barked, panic ricocheting, rage and confusion colliding in the air like static.

And then… stillness.

Alessandro doesn't move. He only presses the barrel harder against Matteo's forehead, as if deciding whether to end it right here. But I know he sees the countdown. It pulses across the screen like a throbbing vein, each second not a threat, but a vow. A slow, deliberate unveiling of everything he's tried to bury, poised to go public.

"What the fuck is this?" he growls.

I don't move. Not even when Matteo's eyes lock onto mine. And there it is, that flash of fear. Not for himself. Not for the gun pressed to his head. But for me.

"You shoot me or Matteo," I say slowly, "and your entire world burns. Every kill order. Every dirty cop. Every bloodstained dollar, every hidden account, it all goes live. You're entire fucking kingdom exposed. Every enemy you've ever made will pick your bones clean before the sun rises."

He goes deadly still.

Even his soldiers falter, a flicker of hesitation bleeding into their eyes. They feel it. The shift. The threat. The moment the ground starts to crack.

"You're bluffing," Alessandro growls. But his voice isn't steady. It wavers, just a fraction. Enough for me to smell the fear bleeding through the cracks in his control.

I tilt my head, eyes locked on his like I'm daring him to fucking move.

"Try it," I say. "Kill him, and everyone finds out. All of it."

He doesn't lower the gun. It stays pressed against Matteo's forehead, his finger twitching on the trigger. But I see it. The hesitation. The crack. The tremble hiding beneath the monster.

Good. Let him feel what it's like to lose control.

"You kill either of us," I go on, taking a few more steps forward, steps that feel steadier than I am inside, "and the countdown ends. Everything goes live. Emails. Videos. Bank records. The whole fucking house of cards comes tumbling down." My voice shakes, but I force it steady. Because Matteo's watching me as though I'm the last thing holding him together, the only thread keeping him from unraveling completely. And I can't let go. Not now.

Alessandro's eyes narrow. I see the exact moment the truth lands. The second he realizes I'm not bluffing. That I'd rather burn it all down than let him walk away with the win. And that scares him more than any bullet ever could.

Matteo shifts slightly on his knees, and the corner of his mouth lifts into that cocky, reckless smirk. The one that used to drive me crazy, the one that still fucking gets me.

Even with death breathing down his neck, he's looking at me as if I'm the brightest thing to ever blaze through his darkness. As if I just set the world on fire, and he's fucking proud to watch it burn.

I drag my eyes from his, just long enough to meet his father's.

"Let him go," I spit, voice low and shaking with fury. "Or lose everything. Your legacy, your power, all of it. Your fucking choice."

I take another step forward. Silence. His father hasn't moved. Hasn't lowered the gun. He's testing me, daring me to crack.

I tilt my head slightly, eyes locked onto his, letting the seconds drip like blood from an open wound. Every heartbeat that passes ratchets up the tension, and I know exactly how much it's fucking killing him to stand still. To hesitate. To let a girl he once saw as powerless hold him hostage.

I stand there, not backing down, every inch of me alive with the weight of this moment. His hand trembles, just a fraction, as he grips the gun tighter. His eyes flash with that sick, twisted pride he's always had in controlling everything.

I let my gaze drop to the phone in my hand, like I've got all the time in the world.

"Eight minutes," I say, voice flat, disinterested.

"You really think you can outsmart me, girl?"

I meet his eyes and let a cruel smile twist my lips.

"I think we both know I have," I say, my tone calm. "Because I know you. To prove your power, Matteo would already be dead." I nod toward the gun, still pressed to his son's head. "But here you are, shaking like a coward, dick shriveled, hands trembling, too much of a pussy to pull the trigger."

Fury simmers like acid just beneath the surface, waiting to eat through the last thread of control he's clinging to.

Matteo shifts on the floor, subtle just enough movement to drag my attention. I flick my gaze to him, and I see it. That same feral heat that has always been our language. He's telling me not to stop. Not now. Not when I've got this bastard by the balls. And that smirk... Jesus. That fucking smirk is just another flavor of foreplay. It shouldn't thrill me. Shouldn't make my breath catch, shouldn't hit me with the force of a kiss meant to bruise. But it does.

"You don't understand what you're starting," Matteo's father growls, but there's a tremor in his voice now, as if the weight of what's coming is finally starting to land.

I arch a brow, head tilting with slow, deliberate intent. "Oh, I understand perfectly," I murmur. "I'm not just ending this. I'm ending you. And let's be honest, it's been a long time fucking coming."

He steps forward, eyes alight with that special brand of desperation men like him mistake for power. "You think blackmail's enough?" he spits. "You think that will bury me?"

"I know it will," I say, my voice cold as I close the distance between us. "The second those names go live, your world turns to ash. Every backroom deal, every bought politician, every filthy secret you've ever whispered into the wrong ear. All of it will be out and when the vultures see the king bleeding... they'll feast on your fucking corpse."

His hand jerks slightly, the gun trembling against Matteo. Good. Let the fucker shake. Let the same fear he shoved down my throat for years rot him from the inside now.

I glance at the phone again. "Seven minutes."

His lips peel back in a snarl, face twisted with rage and something darker, something like panic. "Stop fucking counting."

"I'm just giving you fair warning," I say, voice cold, like a scalpel carving straight through his ego. "That's already more mercy than you ever gave Matteo."

My gaze flicks to the body slumped nearby... my father, bleeding out into the cracks of the floor as if he's trying to seep back into the earth and vanish. For half a second, something inside me twists, claws at my gut, begging me to look away.

Even in death, he's still failing me.

My eyes drag back to Alessandro. I meet his stare and hold it like a fucking blade to his throat. "Time's running out. So either kill your own son or let him go. Because in six minutes and thirty-seven seconds, everything goes live."

Still, even after the threat, he doesn't move. Doesn't even breathe.

I take one step forward towards Matteo, owning the space, and I swear the walls hold their breath.

But the room shifts.

Every man in this room is waiting. Fingers still resting on triggers. Sweat beads on their foreheads.

No one moves, no one dares.

They're waiting for a command that isn't coming, from a king already dead, his crown slipping.

CHAPTER TWENTY ONE

MATTEO

I'm on my knees, the cold bite of the gun pressed to my forehead. Blood coats my tongue. Dust grits between my teeth. My arms are pinned back, muscles screaming under fists that won't let go, but I barely fucking feel it.

Because all I see is her.

Emery.

Standing there, a goddamn reckoning. The fury of every storm that's ever swallowed a man whole wrapped in skin and fire. Her eyes are locked on my father, and fuck, I've never seen anything more beautiful. More terrifying.

She's not afraid. She's fucking magnificent. My fucking queen.

Standing in this destruction like it's a red carpet, daring the monsters to take one more step.

This isn't chaos. This is her fucking coronation. Every scar, every scream, every ounce of fire in her veins is her crown.

And fuck, if I wasn't pinned to the floor, I'd be on my knees still worshipping her with my tongue.

I'd start slow, because she fucking deserves that. Mouth on her thighs, hands anchoring her in place, dragging my tongue over every inch until she's trembling. Until her fingers knot in my hair and her breath catches on my name, a broken prayer gasped into the dark.

I'd kiss her as if she's sacred. Lick her the way a sinner chases redemption.

Then I'd fuck her with the kind of devotion that turns need into worship. My goddamn religion carved between her thighs.

The seconds stretch long. Too fucking long and then the pressure eases.

Not all at once.

The barrel drags against my forehead for a beat like it's reluctant to let go, and wants me to remember it was there... then slowly, he lowers the gun.

I don't know how much time has passed. Seconds, minutes. I don't even know if I'm allowed to breathe yet. But something shifts. Loosens. Like whatever's been coiled tight in my chest, ready to snap, finally lets go.

And for the first time since they pushed me to the floor I feel it. A flicker of something dangerous. Hope. That maybe, just maybe, I'll walk out of this room alive.

I stare at my father. He hasn't moved. He's still standing there with the gun gripped tight in his hand, like it's the only thing tethering him to control. His eyes are locked on me, but there's something different now. Something I never thought I'd see in that cold, ruthless gaze.

Fear. The fucker's scared. And it's not me he's afraid of. It's her.

She's already won, and he fucking knows it. Every second that ticks by is a noose tightening around his neck.

"Five minutes," she says. "If you don't move and let us go, everything goes live." Her words don't just hang in the air, they land on him, like bullets hitting center mass. "Get him up," she demands.

My father's jaw ticks. For a second, I think he might refuse. But then, just the slightest nod, and his men spring into action.

Rough hands haul me off the ground. My legs almost give out, blood rushing back into places gone numb, but I hold myself steady.

Emery steps closer, her gaze never leaving my father. "Let him go."

One of the men hesitates, then finally lets go. The second follows, shoving my arms away with a grunt.

My shoulders burn as blood rushes back through my limbs, nerves screaming like they've been lit on fire. I roll my wrists and flex my fingers.

"You think you've won, Matteo?" My father says, his voice scraping the air with caged fury. "You think you can negotiate your way out of this. You're my blood. You will always answer to me."

Something breaks loose inside me. Years of being his puppet, his pawn, of being molded into something I never fucking asked to be. "You're fucking wrong," I say, voice rough, steady. "I will never answer to you again."

His eyes narrow dangerously. "You think you can walk away?" he snarls, stepping forward like he's still got any power left to wield. "From me? From this family? I'll fucking hunt you down, you hear me. You'll spend every second looking over your shoulder, praying I don't find you."

"It's over," I say. "Your fucking grip on me dies right now. It's fucking over. Your threats don't mean shit anymore. And if you ever come near me or Emery again, I'll fucking end you."

He stands there clinging to his delusion of power like it's not already crumbling in his hands.

But I see that tiny crack in the mask he's worn my whole life. He fucking knows. He's lost me.

Emery's hand slides around my arm, steady and firm.

"Come on," she murmurs. "We need to go, Matteo."

We move backwards, my eyes never leaving my father. I can feel the cold weight of the guns still trained on us, every inch of my skin prickling. But that won't stop me because I'm done playing the obedient son. I'm done bleeding to earn love that was never real.

"Walk out that door," he growls, voice low and vicious, "and you'll never stop running. I'll hunt you down. I'll destroy every fucking inch of the life you think you're building. It will be gone."

I laugh, because the mistake isn't walking away. The mistake was letting that piece of shit shape me into his heir.

Emery's hand tightens around mine, like she knows I'm one wrong breath away from storming back in there, ripping his fucking head clean off. Her grip is the leash holding back the animal in me, the only thing tethering me to sanity right now.

We step through the busted doorway, the goddamn gates of hell finally spitting us out.

The afternoon air hits hard, burning off the filth we just crawled out of, as if the universe itself is trying to scorch us clean.

We move fast. Every step away from that place feels like shedding another layer of pain, of chains, of years spent choking on someone else's idea of who I was supposed to be.

We don't stop moving until we hit the truck, parked deep in the shadows where sunlight barely touches it.

Emery slides into the passenger seat, fast and focused, her chest rising hard, phone still gripped like a loaded weapon.

I climb behind the wheel. My heart's still pounding, too wrecked to realize we made it out alive. For the first time in what feels like a lifetime of bleeding and breaking, I let out a breath.

Not that shallow, panic-laced shit I've been surviving on. A real one.

Emery reaches across the console, her fingers finding mine. "We did it."

"Yeah," I say, voice shredded, thick with emotion. "You fucking did it. You saved us."

She shakes her head. "We saved each other," she says, quiet but certain.

But I know my father. Today's just the prologue to the next fucking nightmare.

He'll come for her. Hunt her down with that rabid-dog smile and blood still drying under his nails. And when he's done tearing her apart, he'll drag my ass back—not because he wants me, but because I'm the fucking heir. Because I'm his, and he won't let anyone forget it. Because control is the only goddamn language that bastard speaks.

A shrill beep slices through the silence. The ten-minute timer detonates like a goddamn bomb.

My eyes snap to hers.

"Did you just leak that?"

Her mouth curves into that wicked little smirk that always meant trouble. Danger laced in sugar.

"Yes," she says. "Matteo, we were never going to be free. Not while he's still breathing. He'd hunt us forever. But now?" She shrugs, casual, effortless, like she didn't just strike a fucking match and torch the world behind us. "Now he won't show his face again."

Emery didn't just threaten my father. She played him. Out maneuvered the monster. And I know exactly what it means.

He'll vanish into the shadows, tail tucked between his legs. His enemies will smell the blood in the water and circle like sharks. Every skeleton he's buried, every bribe, every bullet, every dollar-stained red will all be exposed now. The empire he spent a lifetime building. Gone in a fucking heartbeat. All because of her.

She's chaos wrapped in silk. A fucking storm I'd let wreck me again and again.

Perfect. Deadly. Mine.

I lunge before thought can catch up, fisting her hair and crashing my mouth to hers. The kiss isn't soft. It's teeth and heat and the desperate press of everything we nearly lost. She gasps into me, her body a live wire against mine. Nails digging through cotton like she wants to peel me open and climb inside.

She tastes of freedom. The end of a fight I never thought I'd win. Every fucked-up dream I ever had of coming home.

When I tear my mouth from hers, we're both wrecked, breathing hard, eyes burning, lips swollen with truth we haven't said yet.

"Where to now?" she whispers.

I drag my thumb across her mouth, still tasting her there.

"Anywhere," I rasp. "Anywhere we fucking want. As long as you're mine to fuck, fight, and bleed for."

Because in this moment, with the blood still drying on my skin, I finally get the one thing I never believed I was worthy of.

Her. Every part of me is hers. Has been all these years. Will always be. Even if the world tries to rip her from my arms again, I'll fucking burn it down before I ever let her go.

I turn the key. The engine roars to life, loud and furious, then slam my foot down hard, gravel spitting behind us.

It's just me and her, and whatever the fuck comes next.

Because this is where it starts, my story, not his, not theirs. And I'll bleed, burn, and fucking kill for it if I have to. Because I'm done being written out of my own ending. The one I've always deserved.

EPILOGUE

MATTEO

One Year Later

Some things never fucking change. Like the stars. Still there when you're flat on your back, staring up at a sky that couldn't care less what you've done. Emery curls into my side, meant to be there, born to be the calm that quiets the storm in me.

It almost feels as if we're seventeen again. Just two kids in an empty field, pretending the chaos didn't own us. Her fingers used to trace constellations across the sky like they were maps to something better—as if she could rewrite the universe just by reaching high enough. Rewrite us.

Now the world's finally burning the way it always should've.

After the files dropped. After it went viral.

Every dirty secret my father ever buried was dragged screaming into the light. Politicians collapsed. Dirty cops were exposed. And every bastard who ever played God with our lives went down in a blaze of viral fucking justice.

My father's name lit up the screen. The whole damn world saw what that blood cost.

I don't know where he is now. And I don't fucking care.

We made it out.

One brutal, hard-earned year later, here we are. Lying beneath the same stars that once felt a million miles away. Only now, freedom isn't a whispered dream. It's real.

It's breath that doesn't taste of blood and fear. It's skin-to-skin. It's this. Us.

And fuck, it feels good. The kind of good that feels stolen from a future I never believed I'd be allowed to touch.

Emery shifts beside me, her hand gliding over the soft curve of her belly. It's swollen. Beautiful. Everything. That one small gesture kills me in the best way, because I can see it—the way she already loves our daughter. Fierce and quiet, like fire burning with purpose.

"I still can't believe this is real," she whispers, eyes turned skyward like maybe the stars finally answered her.

I press my lips to her hair. "Believe it," I murmur, voice rough. "It's ours, Emery. All of it."

She turns toward me, eyes soft but still burning with that familiar fire. "Do you ever think about back then? When we were just kids, staring up at the stars?"

I exhale slowly, like I'm trying to breathe out all the years I spent without her.

I tighten my arms around her, pulling her closer, as if I hold her tight enough, gravity won't let go.

"Every damn day," I rasp. "That's how I made it through. Every broken night, every fucked-up piece of me, I held onto you. Even if it was just a memory. Even when it hurt like hell."

Her fingers come up to trace along my jaw, soft and sure.

"I missed you," she says. "Even when I swore I didn't. Even when I told myself I hated you... it was always a lie. I was always yours. Even when I didn't want to be. Even then."

I drag my thumb across her cheek, slow and reverent, as if this is a prayer I never learned the words for. As if touching her is the only way to remind myself she's real and mine.

"You're everything, Emery," I whisper, stripped bare. "Always have been."

My eyes drift down to her stomach, to the life we created from the ruins of who we used to be. Pride hits me so hard it almost hurts.

"I never thought I'd deserve something this good," I admit, voice fraying. "Not with what I've done. Not with the blood on my hands."

She takes my hand and places it over the softest part of her belly. And then... fuck. That flutter. That tiny, perfect movement.

It wrecks me.

"You're going to be an incredible father, Matteo," she says, steady and sure while I'm coming undone. "You deserve this. Every part of it."

I swallow hard. There were days I didn't think I'd live to see another sunrise, let alone this.

I shift closer and kiss her slow.

"I promise you," I breathe against her lips, "I'll tear the fucking world apart before I let anything touch either of you."

Emery leans in, breath trembling between us.

"I believe you," she whispers, and I can see she means it. She knows.

We lie in silence, wrapped in a peace we never thought we'd earn. Emery traces slow patterns on my chest, pausing where time left its scars.

"You ever wonder what our daughter will be like?" she asks, voice dipped in fragile hope, the kind that only surfaces when you stop expecting the world to ruin everything.

I glance down, and that same fierce love slams into me all over again. "Like you, I hope," I say. "Brave. Smart. Strong in the ways that matter."

She lets out a quiet laugh. "She'll have your stubborn streak."

I kiss her temple. "Then God help us both."

Her laughter tears through the night, sudden and bright, splitting the dark the way daylight rips through a storm.

Wild. Free.

She tucks herself into me like this is the only place that's ever made sense.

"I hope she finds this one day," she murmurs, her words brushing against my skin. "I hope she has someone who loves her this fiercely. Someone who'd burn the world down just to keep her safe... the way you did for me."

I stare up at the sky, counting stars like I did as a kid. Searching for something to believe in. I'm not drowning anymore. I'm breathing.

I press a kiss into her hair. This girl. This fucking girl. The one who broke me open with nothing but her truth. Who made me believe in something bigger than survival. In a world where love isn't weakness.

So I hold her tighter. Anchor us to this moment. To this love. To the promise written in every scar we carry.

To the thought of my daughter.

God—it breaks something open in me every time I think it.

I can't wait to meet her.

To hold her tiny body in my arms and whisper the truth before the world ever gets the chance to lie to her.

To tell her she is enough. That she is powerful. That being herself will always be more than enough.

She'll never have to bleed to be believed. Never have to fight to earn her worth. I'll make sure of it.

With Emery by my side, we'll give her the kind of love that builds instead of breaks.

I want to be the kind of father who doesn't just protect her, but sees her.

Who listens.

Who makes space for every wild, impossible dream she dares to chase.

She can be soft or sharp, loud or quiet, bold or afraid, and she'll always be loved. Every single piece of her. We'll give her the world. And we'll teach her how to set it on fire if it tries to take anything away.

ISBN-9781923416079

Also By Eve

Broken Oasis Series

Five Summers
Sixty Days Of Summer
Seven Lost Summers

Standalone

Cruel Intentions

Love this story? Don't miss what's coming next.

Join the Eve Campbell Readers Group : www.facebook.com /groups/9153830006946541

Or Sign Up For My Newsletter : https://subscribepage.io/ wi8Q5T

Follow me on social media for teasers, behind-the-scenes, and daily chaos:

Facebook: www.facebook.com/Evecampbellauthor
Instagram: www.instagram.com/eve_campbell_author/